Meet **Six Characters** *in Search of* **Salvation**

Jessica feels broken and vulnerable from the sudden death of a dear friend. The pre-med student draws solace from her new husband **John**, and yet his love cannot fill this void. So he sacrifices his daily needs to give her a potential balm… and strange things start to happen. Mysterious, mystical things. Things you can't explain….

Jason lives each day clinging to the past. He shuns retirement, seeing no future outside his downtown pet shop, and yet the 70-year-old knows this world will not stand still for him or his longtime veterinarian friend, **Pepper**. Then Jason befriends a lost child, one who turns their lives upside-down….

Bridget finds herself locked in a dark room, with no memory of who she is or how she got there. Her fight for freedom leaves Bridget even more confused, until a sudden change promises a world of happiness. But this paradise, she soon discovers, might just be a prison….

Charles wanders the streets and alleys, hoping the ties he daily builds with one caring soul may soon win him a home. But just as his opportunity arises, a stranger threatens to unravel all of Charles' plans. And that, he will not allow….

Six characters, each seeking salvation, yet falling short. Or so it seems. Yet goodness and mercy may shine even in tales of murder and mayhem… and nothing is certain when one or more of these characters are not human.

That sets the stage for *God's Furry Angels*, a coming-of-age tale exploring the adventures that refine us, the temptations that divide us, and the divine will that binds us together.

The novel also delves deep into the minds of those most alien of creatures, our ever-curious, ever-irrepressible cats.

Illustrated with enchanting photos by the author, *God's Furry Angels* delivers the kind of feel-good experience you'll look forward to reading in your treasured downtime, around a cozy fire with a pot of tea or mug of cocoa, and out loud to your beloved children. It's a fun adventure for all ages, one you will love to revisit again and again!

God's Furry Angels

By Kirby Lee Davis

God's Furry Angels is a work of fiction.
Names, places, characters, businesses, brands, and incidents
are either products of the author's imagination or used fictitiously.
Any resemblance to actual persons (living or dead), events,
or locales is strictly coincidental.

Text and photographs
copyright 2017, Kirby Lee Davis.

Book design by Kirby Lee Davis.

Published in the United States
for Fashan Books, Tulsa, OK.

Learn more at
www.godsfurryangels.com

Other books by Kirby Lee Davis
include *A Year in the Lives
of God's Furry Angels*

ISBN Number (print): 978-1-54392-367-4

First Printing

1 2 3 4 5 6 7 8 9 10

Dedicated to all who helped
make this a reality...
especially my parents
and family, who endured
my journey down this path;
friends Darren Currin,
Becky Roman,
Darla Knight, and Pat Stone,
who always encouraged me;
and my God,
who makes all things possible.

I should also thank the staff
of the Tulsa Hills Chick-fil-A,
which refilled my tea cup
countless times,
always with a loving smile,
through the many, many
months it took to finish this.
If you're sitting there now,
take a good look around.
You just never know
who's working on a novel.

Chapter One

For six days Jessica quietly bore her grief.

Sebastian had been her closest companion for more than a decade, warming her neck on chill winter nights, nestling on her shoulder or lap when Jessica was too upset to do school work or college papers, swatting her toes when Jessica needed a laugh. His absence left a hole in her heart that drained Jessica's zest for life.

John noticed this, of course, but he didn't know how to heal her wound. He soon had an idea, though, and so he put aside his lunch money for a week. That allowed him to come home from work Friday with a small wooden box bound with a scarlet ribbon.

Jessica accepted it with tears, ashamed that he'd discerned the depth of her hurt, yet touched by his love. Sorting through the nest of soft plastic grass within, Jessica uncovered the ceramic figure of a snow-white cat, contently curled into a silky-smooth ball.

"I know it doesn't replace him," John allowed, "but it's a good reminder, I think. It looks like him."

His young wife wiped dry her face. "Yes, it does."

"And it's a promise," he continued. "I'll soon make it real."

That made her smile. She knew they couldn't afford to replace Sebastian now; with their strained budget, she couldn't imagine how he'd paid for this. But she didn't blame John for that. It cheered her that he understood what her childhood friend still meant to her – even if John didn't share that love.

Jessica cupped the glassy form in her palm, clutching it close to her breast as she remembered cherished moments with Sebastian from more than half her existence. Then she laid the figurine in the bare spot on the living room's middle bookshelf, where Sebastian had loved to sleep. Again and again she stroked its smooth back, reveling in the touch.

"He looks good there," John agreed.

"I think I'll call him Sebastian," she decided.

"Good," her husband said. "So – what's for supper?"

That night a loud thump woke Jessica with all the chill of a plunge into icy waters. She snapped up from her soft pillow, drawing her knees to her chin for protection, only to realize with a shiver that she needed still more, and so she snatched the covers to her neck – just in case someone was there, lurking in the shadows, gazing upon her in the darkness. Of course, that ripped the sheets off John, but he didn't notice so it didn't matter.

"John!" she whispered. "John!"

Her husband just laid there, his breath wheezing through his throat like a simmering teapot approaching a boil. That seemed almost sacrilegious to Jessica, a break of his sacred vows to ever defend her, so she jabbed him with the palm of her left hand. He shuddered.

"John! What do you think you're doing?"

"Sleeping," he mumbled.

"Why?"

Her unabashed, irritated wonder stumped him.

"Well," he groaned, struggling to lift an eyelid, "it is dark out."

His eye squinted, looked about, verified it was indeed nighttime, then plopped shut once more.

Maybe it's a dream, he hoped. Just a bad dream.

But it was not to be.

"Get up!" she insisted. "There's something out there!"

"Yeah...."

Jessica shoved him again. "Don't you dare go back to sleep, John Michael Ferguson! You go out there! See what it was."

Her husband grimaced. After three happy, relatively calm months of marital bliss – except for Sebastian, of course – the odds had favored this sort of thing happening sooner or later. Still, he had hoped a few more seasons would pass before Jessica started acting like a wife.

"What *what* was?" he whispered, rolling sluggishly around.

Through the darkness, he found his 22-year-old bride cringing beneath the sheets, her timid eyes glowing in the faint light, her long auburn hair flowing about her silky shoulders like a wondrous waterfall.

It reminded him just why he'd married her. She was a lovely nut.

"What *what* was?" he repeated, a fond humor tainting his voice.

"That sound," she said, surprised he had to ask. "From the living room, I think. Something fell down. The floorboards creaked."

"Well... I don't hear anything now."

"Of course not! Whatever it is knows we're listening now! It's waiting for us to give up and go back to sleep. So, go out there and get them – now!"

"Them?"

"Them – him – I don't know!"

"What about a 'her?' Or 'it?'"

"Ugh!" she exclaimed, kicking him with her left foot. "My father was right about you!"

John couldn't help laughing as he rolled out of bed. Probably a picture fell off the wall, he quietly decided. Even so, he paused to slip into his robe before he stepped with caution to their bedroom door and the blackness beyond. It was best not to take any chances.

"Be careful," Jessica whispered.

There was a strange stillness in the house. Creeping into the bathroom, John felt the darkness clinging to him, weighing upon his skin as might a cold fog. It made him uneasy, almost nervous. That sensation gnawed at him. It was a familiar one... the almost unconscious knowledge that something was there, stalking him.

Passing through the bathroom, he reached the door to the kitchen. There he gazed in, finding no surprises. Even so, he paused out of habit, half-fearing Sebastian would pounce on him at any time.

"That's it," he whispered in sudden revelation. That's what he'd been expecting.

You see, as soon as John and Jessica had started dating, her jealous old cat made a firm point of ambushing John, especially at night. John shuddered, recalling the time right after their honeymoon when that fat beast dropped onto John's head from the top of the refrigerator, sinking his claws into John's pajama top even as the feline's plump waist carried him into a freefall against the oak floorboards. John grimaced at the memory of those scars, though the lingering echoes of Sebastian's thud still cheered him. As did the image of that cat flinging itself off the bookshelf, intent on digging its sharpened claws into John's back, only for John to unexpectedly bend down to finger a loose nail in the floor. He treasured that scene – hearing a distressed howl, glancing up to see Sebastian's broad white underbelly soaring over his head to collide with the closed front door. That alone made up for the hundreds of frustrating times that blasted cat just appeared from the darkness to break John's skin with tooth and claw, then disappear.

Before they'd even gotten married, John had learned to walk these rooms ever alert, like a creeping jungle soldier wary of traps and snipers. That, he realized, was what he was doing now.

Sighing, John passed by the pantry door to the kitchen entryway. The back door and windows were locked tight. Then he checked the dining room, glowing gray-blue from the moonlit window. Beyond the table opened their living room. Looking in, John was surprised to see the front drapes swinging free from their bindings. That hadn't happened since Sebastian's last rampage. John gathered the curtains and tightened their rope knots, then checked the doors and windows. Everything seemed secure.

Confident their small rental home was okay, he took one last look about. Moonlight flooded the living room from the entry window, sparkling against the bookshelf. The figurine lay in its center, playfully rolled onto its back.

On its back?

Two

The next day seemed normal enough. John went back to work, happy to have money for lunch once again, while Jessica, who would soon take the summer off from college, settled into her housekeeping chores. Each time she passed through the living room, she'd give her new figurine a gentle pat, and after that, she'd often pause to gaze out the front window. She could see Sebastian's grave from the windowsill, its grassy top basking in the sun.

It was a lovely spot they gave him to rest in, among the lilacs and daffodils under the spreading elm. The windowsill was pleasant, too, especially when the sun rose over the shady oaks to shine its warmth into the house, as it did then. Jessica recalled Sebastian taking to the spot at first sight, sitting there to brush his long silver fur and gaze out upon the outer world. The wood still carried his scent, though she didn't realize that, and there were other, more visible reminders – like

the claw marks where Sebastian had stripped away most of the wood's smooth finish. But that no longer bothered her. She would often come to stand there, thinking of him, sometimes saying a prayer, then continuing on with her work.

It was during one of those pauses that Jessica noticed the new holes in her curtains – long, streaking runs like those Sebastian used to make when he'd take one of his irritating slides down the fabric, only to bound away laughing when she'd come yelling at him.

Jessica pulled the pale brown curtains out of their bindings, studying these latest scars. The tears did indeed look like claw marks – yet that made no sense, unless these were old, long forgotten slashes. Jessica didn't want to accept that (she had the mind of a steel trap, she liked to tell John, which he'd often add was rusted out or needed oiling), but it was the only logical answer she could see. And the holes did resemble those her gregarious tabby would have left.

She could picture that in her mind... his broad, serpentine snout twitching from side to side, his extended ears frozen at alert, his long, speckled fur at attention, knots and all, as his tail spun itself into a corkscrew. When he was sure the time was just right, the primed muscles in Sebastian's wiry frame would strain against the barrel of a belly born of the lazy life most women provide their cats, and he would attempt liftoff. He'd miss orbit, of course, but make the high peaks of their curtains, which would please him since that had been his objective anyway. He would hang there, dug in, waiting until Jessica or John would enter the room. At that point the arrogant cat would pull in his rear claws, allowing his imposing bulk to drag his front nails through the fabric like scissors through paper. And he'd count off how long he could fall before they realized what he was doing and chased after him. The longer the better.

The thing was, Jessica had been sure she'd seen all of his claw marks – not only on the curtains, but the paneling, the door moldings, the wall trim... everywhere her frustrating yet beloved feline had decided to taunt them. The curtains, in particular, she had watched because they'd cost a lot of money to replace, as John often reminded her in his insistent, husbandly way.

That made her take a deep breath. *When he sees this*...

Sighing, she rebound the curtains with their rope ties, trying to hide the new runs. Yet it pleased her, remembering Sebastian.

That night John came home happy, which also pleased her. He said nothing of the curtains, which pleased her even more. But as the moon entered their bedroom window, Jessica's suspicions awoke her. The loud crash from the dining room had helped, of course.

"John!" she snapped, yanking the sheets around her. "Wake up, John!"

This time he had less trouble breaking his slumber. Practice makes perfect, you know. So with a yawn, he mumbled, "What now?"

"Get up! I heard something."

"Again?"

"Yes, again! You think I'd make something like that up?"

"Well," he yawned, having never thought about it, "I don't know."

"You don't know!?!"

Only then did he realize he'd said something wrong. "Now I do."

"Good. Then get up, John Michael Fergus – "

"Now what's with this saying my full name out loud like it's some sort of guilt proclamation? I do happen to know my name, you know. I was born with it."

"Yes, I know."

"And if I ever forget, it's on my driver's license, my Social Security card, our marriage license – "

"I know!"

"So I don't need you to remind me, dear."

"John, I heard something!"

"Again?"

"Now honey, I've already answered that – *haven't I.*"

"Yes, dear," John acknowledged. So he crawled once more into his robe and staggered about the house, keeping himself in the center of the floor just in case Sebastian tried to snag his toes. And once again John found nothing, although the dining room chandelier was swinging in an odd pattern, as it used to when that crazy cat would leap for the spiders that inevitably nested there. The curtains also hung free – with moonlight glowing through what looked like a new set of running holes.

Aggravated, John almost yelled at the blasted cat. *But it couldn't be Sebastian,* his weary mind realized. *No, it couldn't....*

Regaining his rest was difficult, though eventually sleep did come. Yet the puzzle plagued him. Sebastian stalked his dreams, fading in and out of every image, every thought.

That rascal's still here, John decided.

He awoke to the smell of hot muffins and coffee. Scrambling to get ready for work, John rambled into the kitchen to kiss his beautiful Jessica before getting to what troubled his heart.

"Honey," he asked, fixing his collar, "have you adopted that alley cat?"

"No... why would you think that?"

"Well, I told you the curtains were pulled out again. There are new tears on them, too. Just like Sebastian used to do."

Jessica took a deep breath. John felt her apprehension.

"I have fed him," she admitted, pouring them both a cup of java, "but that's it. I'd be afraid to let that cat in without getting him washed and dipped. And his shots. And we can't afford that."

Actually, the thought of that spotted garbage can veteran prancing about their house just plain bothered Jessica. He seemed a friendly enough cat, but he wasn't gentle. How could he be, having lived in the wild all this time? Even if he somehow were made perfectly clean and flea-free, with an exemplary veterinary record, Jessica wouldn't want that scarred brawler inside her home.

"Well," John said after a long drink, "that's what I'd thought. But it doesn't make sense."

"I think they're old tears," she told him, bringing the muffins and butter to the table. "They must be, dear."

John thanked her again for breakfast. Splitting a hot muffin with his knife brought forth the invigorating scent of warm blueberries. A dash of margarine and, voilà! Near heaven for his nose and tongue! Grateful for his meal, John savored every bite, thanking God he had such a passionate cook for a wife. But not even that welcome glow could dislodge his wary caution.

"I mean, what else could it be?" she continued. "You don't think it's a ghost, do you?"

"No, not a ghost. But something."

That thought hung on both their minds as John left. With a hug and kiss, he slipped out the front door to almost stumble down the steps, pausing beneath the elm as if perplexed. Only as he restarted his walk to work did Jessica realize he had been staring at Sebastian's grave.

She too watched the sun's rays embrace the flowers and soft grass-covered mound, its blue-green leaves swaying gently in the breeze. With a sigh, she lowered herself to the floor, taking comfort in the warm morning. At her elbow

rested the curled porcelain figurine, laying on its side against the bare wood of the windowsill, its outstretched legs glowing in the welcome light.

"Well, hello!" Jessica exclaimed, taking the shiny white miniature in her palm. Stroking its smooth back, she asked, "How did you get over here, Sebastian?"

Uttered without thinking, the question summoned revelations as mysterious as the midnight sounds. How had this sleeping figurine gotten off the bookshelf? She hadn't moved it, and she knew John wouldn't touch it. Being a man, she doubted he even remembered it existed.

How had it ended up on the windowsill?

Returning the ceramic to its shelf, Jessica unfolded the curtains. There she found still another set of scars – the ones John must have discovered.

A cold, nervous chill ran from her fingertips. Wrestling with the tension, she let the silky brown curtains fall back in place.

"What's going on here?" she pondered aloud.

Three

John found his wife sitting on their cat-scratched couch, watching the bookshelf. She had been there off and on most of the afternoon, maintaining a bewildering vigil on the figurine.

It hadn't moved in all that time – a fact that had Jessica asking herself, *Why should it? It's not alive!* And yet Jessica could see no other answer to all these riddles. A porcelain cat that's curled up on the bookshelf one minute, lying on its side in the windowsill the next. Floorboards that creak of their own accord. Curtains that bear new scars each morning. A swinging chandelier – for no reason.

The figurine must have been stretched out when you got it, her conscience told her steel-trap mind. *You remembered it wrong.*

Yet how could she forget something like that in but a day? She was an exobiology student preparing for medical school – her memory wasn't that bad!

This made no sense!

You moved it without thinking, her evaluating side continued. *Or John did.*

Yet John wouldn't do something like that. That would be pervading Jessica's domain. He wouldn't even think of it. And she hadn't moved it – of that she was positive.

You just forgot. These things are all coincidental. You're making something supernatural out of nothing.

That would be the easy answer, wouldn't it? But that left Jessica more uncomfortable than the other solutions, however unrealistic they seemed.

"So what am I going to do?" she asked herself as the setting sun drew near. "Tell John that little critter is alive? Haunted? He'll think I'm crazy – that's what he'll think."

She sank into the worn pillows of the couch. "Maybe I am."

Maybe you are, replied her conscience. *This isn't exactly scientific.*

Jessica didn't care. Science couldn't answer everything. Much in this world defied description or explanation.

Well then, continued the argument, *look at it this way: What would Christ think of this? How would He explain it?*

That stumped her. None of this seemed biblical – a realization that made her question her sanity anew. But as she sat there, pondering it in that light, the situation no longer seemed so clear. Didn't the Bible have its mystical elements? Priests turning rods into snakes? Demons occupying pigs? A donkey that talked?

So how would that figurine serve God?

"How indeed?" she wondered, giving free rein to His wondrous ways.

That made her ask another question: Why should all this scare her? The little kitten hadn't done anything terrible. It was just playful, like Sebastian had been.

That fact stopped everything. It was indeed acting just like Sebastian had.

For some reason that filled Jessica with joy.

That's how John spied her through the window – relaxing on the couch, wondering what he would say when she explained how her beloved cat had returned to her in the form of a glassy figurine.

But she never got the chance.

She first heard the timid calls before her husband came through the door. Then she saw the large box in his hands, the white and tan paws stretching their claws through the holes, and she understood. Jessica threw herself around John before the screen door could slam shut, hugging him so tight that he almost dropped the box. A frightened whine penetrated its walls.

John held her close, nuzzling her neck, her ear. "This is how to end a hard day's work," he whispered with much love. "But you'd better take this first."

Even as he handed her the box, the kitten was squeezing her brown, gray, and white spotted head through the folded lids. Jessica opened the cardboard crate and drew the curious feline to her neck, snuggling her between her left shoulder and cheek. The kitten squealed and struggled to escape, but as she felt the love surrounding her, all resistance ended. A loud purring filled the room, and Jessica's heart.

"Oh, John! She's so beautiful!"

Her husband smiled, slipping out of his coat. This sight alone made it all worthwhile.

Jessica rocked back and forth, cuddling the contented kitten to her cheek, beaming to the world her happiness. Only as John lifted the small bag of cat sand from the box did the reality of this strike her.

"But, John," she whispered, "I thought we'd agreed... we can't afford another cat right now. Not with our budget and all."

"Yeah, well, maybe so," he allowed. His eyes fell on the figurine on the shelf, its face staring at their newcomer. "But I figured this house just isn't right without one. I'll start packing my lunches for the summer; that should free up some money."

"Oh, John!" Was there any doubt why she loved him?

"She's had all her shots, you know, so that saves us some from what we'd budgeted. They gave us some worm medicine. And she was on sale, too. They were practically giving her away!"

"Oh, dear, John. You don't think there's anything wrong with her, do you?"

John leaned over and stroked the velvety fur under the kitten's chin. She lifted her head, allowing John to roll his fingers along her throat. Her purring deepened.

"I think," he began, "that you'd better start thinking of a name."

"Oh, that's easy," proclaimed Jessica. Pulling the kitten to her face, she whispered, "Isn't it, Bridget?"

With a tinny meow, Bridget swiped her left paw at Jessica's nose. Jessica laughed.

John was right, she decided. The house did seem better now.

By Kirby Lee Davis

Four

So Bridget found her home at the young Ferguson household, in the hearts of a struggling accountant and a promising pre-med student. Jessica soon learned there was nothing wrong with the inquisitive kitten, although John harvested more doubts each day. But then, he had never bothered to find out why the rambunctious feline had come so cheap. If he had, with the memories of Sebastian still fogging his mind, John might never have picked Bridget.

Like you, he thought the small spotted kitten's tale began with her pinched head squeezing out of her box. Actually, it started the same day Sebastian died. Indeed, this adventure began that very moment – for as Jessica's aged protector breathed his last, the elderly owner of Jason's Pet Store slid his creaking front door open on his way home after a hard day's work. There in his dusty entryway sat a crumpled brown paper bag, its squashed base swaying back and forth.

Now Jason Alexander Scabbard had many reasons to ignore the discarded bit of trash that cluttered his storefront. He was tired and hungry, having forgotten to pack his lunch, and the walk home promised to be a long, hot one. But there was more to it than that. Jason was worn out. Five years past retirement, he still put more than 60 hours a week into a one-man business that rarely ever paid his bills. Jason had to do this, for no one else cared enough about his shop to keep it alive. Oh, Jason knew most people preferred those big pet supermarkets, but he couldn't just abandon the old brick and mortar heritage of downtown. He had worked the area for more than 50 years, as his father had before him. It was part of the community! It meant something, even if other people were too blind to realize it.

With stubborn pride, Jason resisted everything to do with the modern world. He clung with fondness to his horse-hair broom, two-speed fan, dial phone (even if it no longer worked), and his 1930s typewriter-keyed, bell-clanging brass cash register. Jason treasured the sound it made, a pleasant ring that echoed through his life. But even more, he harbored a deep love of animals large and small. Each day it saddened him to find more and more neglected and mistreated dogs and cats... some left outside on hot days without shade and fresh water, others living

from trash dumpsters, often abandoned by thoughtless people who lost their love for their pets once these poor beasts grew out of their infancy. More than anything, Jason made it his mission to care for those forgotten creations of God. So when he saw that rolled-up bag, and heard the weak moans coming from its thin walls, Jason didn't hesitate. Lifting it with a loving touch, he went back into his shop and called his oldest friend, Pepper James.

"Pep," he yelled into the receiver, "you still there?"

"Would you be talking to me if I wasn't?"

"Now, Pep, I was just afraid of interrupting your supper."

"Since when has that ever stopped you?"

Jason chuckled. "When I thought you'd invite me over!"

"Oh, har! You eat here more often than you do at your own table, you old skinflint!"

That brought a full laugh, which Jason had to choke off when he felt his false teeth coming free. What was in the bag must have heard them clicking, for it started rambling in his grasp.

"Oh, I'm sorry, little fella!" Jason exclaimed, laying the bag down. He unrolled the crimped paper neck, allowing in the open air. As he expected, a tiny kitten soon stumbled out – a poor little thing, underfed, only a few weeks past opening her eyes. The dogs in the backroom kennel soon smelled the newcomer, raising such a ruckus that the puppies out front just had to join in. The alarmed kitten threw herself back in the bag.

"I'm sorry," Jason said, peering into its dark folds. The spotted kitten huddled against its ragged back, her hair all aflutter, her eyes glowing. "You've got to forgive them," Jason assured her. "They haven't seen you yet, you know."

The phone clattered to life. "Are you still there?" came Pepper's crotchety voice. "What's going on over there?"

"Oh, Pep – I was wondering if you were still there. I need to bring another one over."

"Oh, heckfire, Jason! It's Friday night already!"

"I know, Pep."

"It's Friday night! Margaret's got some stew cook'n!"

"That sounds good, Pep."

"Oh, heckfire! I mean – oh, agh! You big, blundering, bubble-brained... you can't just bring me every little critter you find hurting in the world, Jason! You

can't do it! By golly, Jason, you really irk me! What's it been, now, 38 years? Yes, it has – 38 years, Jason! For 38 years... no, that's *39* years! For *39 years*, Jason, you've been bringin' me every dang stray you've been able to latch your itchy little fingers on – but no more. No more, I tell you! You can keep your birds and cats and poodles and frogs and turtles and skunks and lizards and birds and stuff! I can't afford to do it anymore! I'm tired, Jason, tired – and Margaret's got some stew simmerin' and I'm hungry and it's Friday night and I'm going home. Now! I'm already out the door and gone, so don't call me again!"

"OK, Pep. I'll be right over."

"Oh, you kill me. Do you know that? You kill me."

"She shouldn't need more than some vitamins, and maybe some worming and a good dip."

"Oh, heckfire, Jason. All right. Just get over here quick, will you?"

"Sure, Pep. Tell Margaret I'll want cream with my cornbread."

So Jason walked the three blocks over to Pepper's crumbling veterinary hospital, where his childhood friend did all he could to help jumpstart the little kitten back to health. After a vitamin shot and a treat, Margaret came downstairs to give Bridget a gentle bath, killing her fleas and three miserable ticks. Jason then carried her back to his shop, all to let her gather her rest through the night within his pen of nine other kittens. Jason didn't even wait to taste the cornbread and stew – his new little girl was his first priority.

"Now you just rest," he told little Bridget, laying her on a soft pillow among all the other cats. "You'll make plenty of new friends now."

Or so he had thought, until he returned the next morning. That's when the chaos began.

Five

At first light Jason slurped down his cereal, rinsed his teeth, and rambled down the six blocks to his rustic downtown shop, clicking his cane against the old, WPA-era sidewalk the whole way.

That in itself wasn't unusual; he had about 2,000 square feet of dogs, cats, birds,

and fish to feed and let run each morning, plus bedding to change, cages to clean, inventory to count, and supplies to restock. But this Saturday morning was different. More than anything, he really wanted to see how the little kitten was doing.

Sure enough, when he looked into the dusty front window showcase, he found the ten kittens entwined like a yarn ball, snoring, with little more than a paw, tail, ear, or back showing from any one of them. The dogs started their usual welcoming howls as Jason jiggled the lock on his security door, and the puppies and birds chimed in as he fiddled with the rusty keys to his father's original glass door, its pane still smeared from their Depression-era coal stove. By the time Jason set foot into his shop, about half the kittens were prancing about, wide awake and ready to eat. The other half still slept. A five-alarm fire wouldn't have roused them.

Bridget, new to the morning ritual, hung from the wire roof of their cage. Her brown eyes flared wide and wild at the commotion. Her hair shot straight out like porcupine quills, and her tail whipped at anything that neared her.

That's how she remained when Pepper came to visit.

Pep, you see, often helped Jason prepare his shop on Saturday and Sunday mornings. He had the time, since his veterinary office didn't open on weekends except for emergencies, and he liked to assist his life-long friend – though he would never let Jason know how he felt about that. To Pepper, it was just like playing cards. Throwing out used newspaper and washing down cages offered a good time to argue. But this Saturday, Pepper also was curious about how the little kitten was doing, and so he arrived at the front window not too long after Jason himself – just in time to see the other kittens piling up beneath Bridget, trying to grab her tail as it twitched about.

"What'cha doing out there?" Jason called to the veterinarian. "Come on in, Pep! You could've had the canary cages swept by now!"

"Just checking on our little friend," said Pepper, propping open the outer security door.

"Yeah, well, they were all a bundle this morning."

Setting aside his broom, Jason joined his friend beside the kitten cage. Pepper was busy easing Bridget's claws free of the wire bars. She resisted, of course, but with the other kittens swiping at her twisting tail like it was a catnip mouse, it didn't take long for her distractions to get the best of her so that she fell, crashing

into a pile of her comrades. Almost upon landing she was on her feet and scrambling away, leaping to safety on the high back of an overturned pipe covered in old carpet. There she remained, crouched, pawing at anything that moved through the tunnel.

"Looks like she'll be all right," Pepper said with a smile.

"So it does," Jason agreed. "You did a good job – this time."

Pepper shared the laugh.

"You just see that she gets someone who loves cats," the veterinarian said. "If she doesn't calm down, she's going to need it."

So will her master, he knew.

"She's never been around so many dogs before," Jason declared. "I saw it last night. They spooked her, Pep, that's all – all their barkin' and carrying on. Just like when I got here. But she'll get used to it."

Pepper nodded, though not convinced. He'd seen similar anxieties when animals mixed at his office. But sometimes such distress lingered, especially among younger critters.

"Just the same," he urged, "I'd take care with this one. Don't let just anyone buy her."

"Now, Pep! When have I ever done that?"

"Well, you've had me guiding you for 39 years."

"Oh, har to that!"

"But I'm not always going to be here to keep them – and you – out of trouble," Pepper continued, enjoying his boast.

"Well don't you worry about that. You can just scurry back to your little practice and don't worry about those of us who really do something to help these little guys."

"Scurry? Scurry? Why, you! Oh, heckfire! I didn't rise at dawn – "

"Yeah, yeah," Jason interrupted. "Margaret made you get up."

Pepper hadn't finished: " – and rush out the house – "

"Down the stairs." The James family lived in the apartment above their clinic, you see.

" – and run all the way down here – "

"Two whole blocks. And at tortoise speed."

" – just for you to insult me."

"Guilty as charged," Jason gave in, smiling.

"Yes, well, it's about time you realized it," Pepper replied. "Just you do as I say about that kitten."

"Don't you worry. I'll find her a good home, once she settles down some. I might even keep her myself."

But as the day passed, Jason began to have some doubts. Bridget clung to the top of that pipe like a vulture, attacking anything and everything that dared approach her. Only after two hours did she show signs of wearing down, just after he opened the store, but then she discovered the chow bowl and dug in. Renewed, Bridget took to pouncing on each kitten, chasing them around the cage until they submitted beneath her bounding tackles. The customers loved it, though Jason doubted the other kittens shared their laughter. Three times she or her victims knocked over the water pan in their rampaging, and once the chow bowl got rolled across the cage to the sandbox – which soon provided its own challenge. For once Bridget discovered the food, she often returned, crunching down the dry chow with gusto. The other kittens, riled and rounded up in turn, also took to eating more, and so Jason found himself changing the sandbox far earlier than he'd wanted. That proved the one thing able to still his new kitten. With fascination, Bridget watched each time Jason flipped back the cage top to replace the sandbox liner with fresh kitty litter. Both times she insisted on using the sand before he'd even finished securing the bag, and yet her eyes ever remained on his arms, which seemed to reach from the heavens to restore order to her realm.

Jason realized why she watched him so after the sandbox smell demanded a third changing. Bridget tensed as he approached the cage, eyeing him with something close to appreciation. When he raised the lid, she pounced. Jason yanked his arm back, enchanted with her for trying that. Bridget landed like a gymnast on the cage wall and clung there, staring up with wide, alert eyes.

"Oh, you're a bright one!" Jason exclaimed, lifting her with care from the wire to set her atop the carpeted pipe. "Go ahead, little one. Hunt me! I'm glad you're feeling so strong."

Jason changed that view when he gave the sandbox one last changing before closing up. Only then, as he swung open the kitten cage and Bridget leaped out, did Jason realize she'd been trying to escape all along. It took almost a half-hour of crawling through dust balls, picking up shelves dislodged in her wake, and shooing her away from the fish and birds, before Jason managed to corner and apprehend the wild spotted squirt.

That's why he returned home weary and late, her snarls and heckles haunting his every step.

So ended Day One. The feline Houdini got better after that.

Six

S o now you've met Jessica and John, the two Sebastians, Jason, and Pepper. But to truly understand this tale, you have to look into the heart of Bridget. For it is there that all their dreams collide, and their hopes revolve.

Some consider the mind of a cat a most undecipherable thing, a quagmire of selfish ambitions and impenetrable mysteries. True, the beasts don't understand all human speech, or comprehend such intricate life enhancements as catalytic converters, microwave popcorn, or rabbit ear antennas. They don't need to. God blessed them with far more efficient paths of communication. And it is also true that cats don't devote themselves to servitude and submission to a human's every whim, like dogs, for example. That's also unnecessary. They can survive on their own, thank you very much. True, many bond to humans when it suits their purpose – or, like Sebastian, when it is ordained, because the "hairless giants," as cats see humans, could not develop as He wills without a feline influence. But in most cases, a cat will cling to independence, as guaranteed all their kind by the Doctrine of Grakk-koth long, long, long ago.

Yes, that long.

That most humans don't comprehend this or recognize the law doesn't change its validity; it merely shows how much more mankind has to learn about this great big world. Most cats don't care to stress the point. They usually end up going along with the illusion of human ownership since it almost always means a good bed, frequent massages, and regular meals – but it's a convenience of will, nothing more.

Yet cats aren't born fully grasping this, any more than humans come into the world (or even leave it) able to gracefully operate a fountain pen. Cats learn from life, and each other. That's why Bridget reacted as she did. You see, all things –

even humans – harbor that instinct to avoid imprisonment, and yet Bridget was forced into it twice, to great peril. Being shoved by unkind hands into that flimsy bag disoriented her. It subjected her to piercing needles, a humiliating chemical immersion, and a lockdown in cold darkness among other frightened, trembling prisoners. And when sleep finally brought escape, she awakened to that most hideous of fears: being suppressed in a stuffy stone cell amongst a throng of stupid, howling mongrels.

The irony was, whoever cast her into that brown

paper bag ended up doing God's will, for otherwise the little kitten would never have met Jason – and would have missed a destiny on which so many lives teetered.

Even so, everything that followed hung on her responses, her decisions – on what she chose to do, on who she chose to be. And that, of course, is how God always wills it.

At first she panicked. Exasperated, frightened, she leaped upward, seeking escape – only to discover a field of entwined metal strings blocking her way. She clung to it, upside-down, knowing she was confusing everything and caring not a lick for it. She wanted out!

The fellows below called to her. "What do you think you're doing?" asked one black tabby. "That looks fun!" cried a silver long hair. "Don't be afraid!" offered still another. "You can't get out that way!" scoffed someone else. But Bridget (which was not her proper name, mind you, but we won't get into that) didn't care. Desperate and hungry, she

needed time to think, to understand what was going on. So Bridget hung there, pondering it all through the aggravating harping of the wretched canines. And since she ignored the other fellows, she didn't notice the giant hairless one's scabby digits dislodging her back claws until it was too late.

As one might expect, that plunge and impact made Bridget mad. The catcalls didn't help, of course. Some were caring, a few compassionate, but most just wanted to know what she thought she had been doing, hanging up there like a crazy bird. They knew she wasn't hurt – God had molded cats strong and flexible enough that such falls rarely ever bruised them, though it might mess up their fur. But Bridget didn't care about that. Confused, fearful, starving, the last thing she'd needed was a good stout blow to the head. So the kitten sprang up to the highest point she could see, a round mound of some unnaturally thick grass that sheltered a long cave. That spot, Bridget decided, was hers and hers alone. Never again would she let herself be ambushed and imprisoned. From this moment on, she would command.

There she stayed, swatting at every fellow that dared approach her, until her nose decided something she'd smelled all along just might be eatable. So she went to check it out. There, in a shallow bowl of compressed earth, lay what appeared to be dried bites of something made of meat. Chewed, discarded bits lay around; the other fellows obviously had been surviving on this. On that thought alone, Bridget took the risk and ate a piece. She then had another, and another. They weren't savory, or even somewhat pleasant, but they satisfied her hunger.

A fellow drew near. His long gray hair flowed like water about his back legs and chest, but stood upright about his spine and forepaws. That marked a polite greeting, promising assistance, but no intimacy. His ears faced full forward, a wary sign of concern suggesting the fellow did not trust Bridget. His eyes narrowed, tight and focused, showing his alertness centered on her alone. And he offered no words of any kind – a sign he wished no further contact. He wanted food, she stood in the way, and so he was informing her that he would pass by.

Bridget, therefore, bared her teeth, stretched her claws, and charged.

We might all agree that, just perhaps, that wasn't the most courteous response. But look at it from her eyes. Bridget was new to the cage, and still intent on getting out. This young fellow was not new to the cage, or so it seemed. Therefore, she reasoned, he might very well know something about this prison that she didn't – and yet he'd made it clear he didn't wish to speak with her. That left Bridget no

choice but to earn his knowledge and loyalty by conquering him, more or less. She didn't mean to hurt him. She only wished to learn what he knew.

Such logic led her to topple every fellow in the cage. Not one of them knew the answer she sought, though it soon came to her. The hairless giants had some love of the dirt the fellows cleaned themselves in. She used that to her advantage.

The first day's escape proved easy, though it got her nowhere. The metal string cage was but one cell in a larger prison of strange ledges, dusty corners, and deadwood walls – and everywhere she went, she found still other metal string cells, some holding back those stupid mongrels, others containing multihued birds, still others housing some monstrous, fuzzy rats. And then there were the cold, hard walls of towering water that glowed under brilliant suns all their own, revealing swarms of fish that seemed right at her claw tips. That fascinating discovery proved her undoing, for it was as she balanced on a thin ledge above the bubbling water, wondering what would happen to her paw if she stuck it within that mystical pond, that the hairless giant's callused digits fell upon her. Before she knew it, she'd been lifted by the scruff of her neck, suspended high above the world, and dropped back into the cage with the other fellows. She had but caught her breath when the sun went out.

She spent that night atop her mound, thinking. Sounds and scents were starting to sort themselves out, even as darkness and sleep brought activity within the wooden walls to a standstill. From the thick dust and old, permeating smells, this prison appeared ancient. The air just hung there, mixing with the breath, belch, and gaggle of every creature around, but not refreshing itself. Yet sometimes, every now and then, Bridget could remember a sharp, brief current had flowed through the grounds. From her mound, she couldn't identify where this breeze came from, though she could recall its last appearance – when the sun had gone out. That strange rush of night didn't concern her, but something else did. She could no longer smell the hairless one.

As the day opened on the front window, Bridget lay hatching a plan. Sure enough, with the clattering roll of metal came the harpy hounds a'baying. She wanted to cover her ears, but couldn't allow it to break her concentration. Then she heard what she'd recalled – more clatter, followed by the groan of old wood. So she waited, seeking the sign that had trailed the groan.

She waited some more.

And then it came – the rush of fresh, outside air. It invigorated her with the

scent of freedom!

Bridget pondered that sequence of events all through the day. The other fellows often got in the way, of course, testing her as they did, but she concentrated on the sounds and wind. For she now realized escaping the metal strings was only the first obstacle. True freedom lay in figuring out how to get out as the outside air got in. And that was tied to the hairless ones.

She made a point of getting outside her cage twice that second day – once as the giant drew out the cleaning sand, and once as he refilled their food pan. Each time she learned more of the hairless one – the weird imitation skins he wore, the unusual grunts he made when crawling against the deadwood floor, the distaste he had for dust. That last bit made no sense, considering how often he collected the used sand, but it made no difference to how Bridget would find her deliverance. For the central problem remained, in two parts: the gusts never blew when the giant opened their cage, and the giant never ceased to hunt her down once she got out. Therefore, the chance seemed remote that she would be free of the cage when an outside breeze came.

All this changed the third day. As the sun rose high, a series of short gusts came and went, each tied to the groaning wood and renewed moans of the mutts. But this time in the wind's wake were several hairless ones of various shapes, sizes, and smells. They made all sorts of sounds, some soft and cuddly, some apprehensive, and one downright scary in its unrest. At one point the giants drew near the fellows, staring through the metal strings with large, fluttering eyes. Most of them left after a while, but not the littlest one. He stood there, eyes wide, his hairless digits wrapped through the strings.

For some instinctive reason this thrilled Bridget. She didn't understand it, and yet, something about the innocent eagerness flowing out of this little giant intrigued her, as it did the other fellows. One of them, the sandy tabby known among the kittens as Quagloc-karrok – a name that would only get longer as he matured – jumped up beside Bridget, hoping perhaps to get a better view. He was most polite about it, dampening his fur, lowering his ears, and kneeling beside her, all in a bid to show subservience to her post, but Bridget didn't like the distraction and kicked him hard. He rolled and rolled – ending up beside the cub's bare pink digits!

All the kittens hesitated, wondering what in God's Great Plan could possibly follow this. A soft crowing sound drew from the cub. A couple of his digits shifted

among the metal strings to rub against Quagloc-karrok. To Bridget's surprise, the young kitten seemed taken by the move. The fellow pushed his neck and ears against the digits, then licked them! The hairless giant cub squealed, which brought the other giants walking back in their loud, ponderous steps. Bridget tensed, not knowing what would happen. The cage opened. Instinct drove her to leap at this opportunity, but this time the hairless one swatted her aside as if it was the most natural thing to do in the world. Without pause, his large scaly digits pinched Quagloc-karrok behind his ears and lifted the fellow out of the cage. The lid swung shut, even as the struggling kitten was laid in the hands of the tiny giant. As Bridget and all the other fellows watched, the hairless cub wrapped its digits about its brown-haired prize and drew the kitten to its face, all with obvious love. With a brief pause the old wood groaned, and a blast of wind swept about them. At its end, all but one of the giants had disappeared.

Bridget could not believe it, and yet it was true. Quagloc-karrok was gone!

The other fellows were all aflutter over this. "When will he come back?" many pondered aloud. "Where did he go?" "Why didn't they choose me?" "What will happen now?" But most of their discussions turned in anger to Bridget. She was the one who had spilled their food and water, the one who had caused all the havoc with those foolish escapes, the one who had kicked Quagloc-karrok – just as she'd been kicking and scratching them all.

After that, Bridget never enjoyed a quiet moment within that shop. And neither did Jason.

Seven

After one week, Jason had just about had enough.

The constant barrage of barking dogs he could stomach – after all, he had endured it for almost 50 years. But never, ever had he known a cage of kittens could cause such turmoil. Ever since he'd added that little, spotted brat, the levels of hissing, howling, and snapping had risen so high, the birds were beating themselves from wall to wall, the fish were hovering in the far corners of their tanks –

"Even the backroom mutts are skulking," he told Pepper during a morning visit. "Sometimes it's scary, Pep. For the last five days, they've been scrappin' from morning to night. Almost always they're ganging up on the little kid, and yet, I'll tell you, she's probably a match for all of them. They get to rollin' and snappin' hard. Two, maybe three times a day, the whole bundle will get to piling on and shoving, and the whole cage moves. Once it rocked sideways so hard, I thought for sure it was going to topple!"

Pepper could only nod. For the present, things were somewhat quiet. Most of the young cats for sale were huddled together in somber exhaustion, but the little kitten that so concerned his friend was lying atop the carpeted pipe, staring deep into the veterinarian's eyes. It unsettled him – and yet, he couldn't help feeling that he'd experienced all this before.

"She does that every time the door opens," Jason explained, "just leaps up there and waits. Like she's watching to see what we'll do. The others, I think they use the time to regroup, to rest up for their next attack. Sometimes they don't wait long, but sometimes...."

Pepper turned to better hear his friend. A patient man, he was used to biding his time for people who'd paused in mid-thought – which pet owners often did, when discussing their animals. But now he had thoughts of his own, and they hinged on what Jason was thinking.

"Sometimes what?" he asked.

Jason shuffled over to his cash register, checking the funds in the drawer. "Well, I think she's out to get me."

"Get you?"

"Well, yeah. Each day she's managed to get out at least once, and the others, they've started copying her." Jason leaned close to his register, as if to hide behind it. "I think she's teaching them."

"Teaching them?" Pepper exclaimed.

"Oh, yeah! I can't even open that cage now without two or three of them making a break for it."

"That explains the sand pile," Pepper mumbled, as well as the spilled food and dirty water in the kitten cage. All three looked like they hadn't been touched for days.

"Heckfire! I haven't been able to change it since noon yesterday!" Jason said of the sandbox. "Four of them got free then!"

Pepper choked back laughter. "How?"

"Why, they just jump up my arms, like little, clawed jackrabbits! After that first time, I've learned to wear these heavy shirts, or else they'd be cutting me to bits!"

"I was wondering about the flannel." *You must be sweating like a dog*, Pepper thought.

"And when they get out," Jason continued, "all they do is go around knocking things off the shelves, or throwing themselves at the bird cages, or jumping onto the aquarium lights. Two of those troublemakers actually fell into the tanks! Those were two sorry, soaked kitties, let me tell you!"

Pepper couldn't hold back his chuckles any longer.

"Sure, go ahead," Jason snapped. "But it's not funny."

That only made Pepper laugh harder.

"You mean you can't handle a handful of kittens?" he asked.

"These are not ordinary kittens," Jason declared. "And that one," he pointed at Bridget, "she's a monster."

"Oh, come on!"

"Look at her!" Jason demanded. So they did, meeting her intense glare. Pepper wondered if she'd stalk a catnip mouse with such determination.

Again, it all seemed familiar.

"I tell you," said Jason, "you wouldn't want to meet her in a dark alley. If she were German Shepherd sized, she'd be a killer."

"Oh, she just needs a good home, that's all."

"A good home? She needs a tranquilizer the size of a Sherman tank! She's a devil, she is! I should have known, too – finding her at my doorstep in a beat-up paper bag. Someone was out to get me, that's for sure."

Pepper stiffened. "Someone was cruel to one of God's most loving creations, and you helped her. She just doesn't want to be caged, Jason! Look at her. I'll bet that if you'd let her stay out, and befriend her, she'd do wonders for you here."

"Oh, har! You know I can't do that."

"Why not? I'll bet you have your share of mice around here."

"Maybe so, but I couldn't have a cat running free. Forget my fish, my birds – how do you think the other kittens would react, seeing her outside the cage?"

"They wouldn't think anything of it. You sell them too quickly."

Jason wasn't convinced. "And think of the dogs, man! There's no way I could have a free-ranging cat around them."

Pepper started to protest, but then he thought the better of it and said nothing. Jason was probably right about that.

"Well then, you need to sell her," he said, "and quickly."

"Hah! I haven't sold a kitten for five days – ever since they started that scrappin'. Everyone comes in, laughs at the wild wrestling show, and then chooses a nice, quiet goldfish. And neither one of us makes any money on that."

"No, we don't," Pepper agreed with a warm smile. His eyes fell once more on Bridget, just as three other kittens bounded upon the pipe. She cast them off with hardly any effort at all. It made Pepper chuckle. He hadn't seen a cat with such spirit since the Fergusons had brought old Sebastian in. Even with John and Jessica holding him down, that blasted cat had fought his way out of their grasp and threw himself at Pepper's hand. The image of that defiant beast biting through the syringe was one Pepper would enjoy telling Saint Peter, when he had the chance.

"You know," he reflected, "I know someone who might take that kitten."

"Tell me his name," Jason demanded, "and I'll make him a deal he can't refuse."

And that's how John walked home two days later with a new kitten and a week's worth of cat litter, all for the price of a bottle of deworming pills. That's also how Jason avoided a nervous breakdown.

Eight

It took about six weeks for the little kitten to realize that when this quirky pair of mostly hairless ones yelled "Bridget" – or in the case of the hard one, "BRIDGET!" – they were actually talking to her or about her.

She didn't know if she particularly liked the pair of sounds, or the way he usually spoke them, but overall, it seemed an improvement. Sure, it still opened the door for potential misunderstandings, but at least it gave her some indication that she was getting through to them – that they could be taught at least basic tricks, if not ones of limited complexity. Like which foods were a waste of time to

put in her bowl, because she wasn't going to eat them even if they crawled across the room and forced themselves down her throat. Or how these giants had better keep the pillowy couch things arranged the way she wanted if they didn't wish to find the fluffy pads full of holes in the morning.

Of course, she might have figured out sooner what sounds they had linked to her if the two giants had been more consistent. The softer and kinder – if somewhat stranger – one did better at it than the heavy, gruff, stiff-footed one. From what Bridget could tell, that foul-tempered bull mouthed all sorts of awkward, ear-numbing noises toward her in blunt, thunderous pitches – from "Youdarncat!" to "Stopit!" to "Agh!" and "Getdownfromthere, youfleabag!" Once in a while, he included her appointed title. The more feminine one, however, almost always referred to her with the slurred, two-syllable "Bridget," using soft, gentle tones that inferred love over all things.

It was strange, adjusting to it all. Bridget had been terrified when that old hairless giant had trapped her in that dark cardboard box. All her schemes for deliverance – dashed, just like that! But then she'd heard the groan of old wood, felt the thrilling rush of fresh air through the box holes, and all her perceptions changed. This wasn't the hell she'd feared – she was being taken away, just like Quagloc-karrok! This hairless one was carrying her to freedom!

Yet that perception itself faded as realization settled around her. The stuffy box confined her tighter than did the metal string cage, she was all alone in its shadowy hold, and the only wisps of light and liberty available to her were jiggling glimpses from the paw-sized holes in the walls. Through them she witnessed brief, bouncing images of all sorts of exotic, dreamy things – leafy wooden statues that stretched far above the giants to dance in the breeze high above their heads; even larger, multicolored deadwood constructs with shiny transparent walls; field after field of green, green grass, and an endless turquoise sky. The topsy-turvy views stirred her, but as each experience built upon the next, the thrill of them grew shallow, losing substance against the reality of that dreary box. Despair crawled along her spine with each plodding step the giant took. She didn't know where she was going. She had no way out. This wasn't freedom – it was disaster!

As her patience dimmed, she caught the familiar strains of old wood flexed and stressed. Fears of another metal string cage overwhelmed her. In frustration, she threw herself against the walls, and found a seam in the box. With practiced tenacity, she forced her face through – only to find still another surprise. This was not the hairless giant's dusty prison of hellhound howls! The air was fresh and quiet, the walls far apart and wide open, and there wasn't a cage in sight!

So overcome with relief was Bridget, she didn't notice the long, gentle digits that scooped her up – but the love that flowed from that embrace overwhelmed her. For the first time ever, Bridget sensed within herself the passion Quagloc-karrok found when she had kicked him into the grasp of the tiny giant. From deep in her heart, she purred contentment.

Bridget still remembered the joyous discovery of caressing the feminine giant's soft neck, only to find this hairless one wasn't hairless – she wore a surprising crown of long, auburn tresses! Bridget flicked at the thick hanging strands with her claws, drawing warm laughter from the giant, and so she clutched at them again. It thrilled the depths of her being. How she loved sitting on that broad shoulder, hearing the joy that brewed from the giant's heart to echo through her throat! Not so hairless after all! Bridget laughed. But then her claws snagged a clump of the brown locks. Just that quickly the female giant tensed and the other one laughed, which made the female darken even more. Yet never did it cloud the love within her.

That, Bridget soon learned, was the difference between the Jessica giant and the John giant. Even though the male may have rescued the kitten from the mongrel horde, John often didn't seem to care if she were there or not. This confused her. For while the Jessica female reflected warmth in her touch, intonation, and body contours, the John male often ignored Bridget's presence, only to turn stormy without warning.

Like the time when Bridget crossed the deadwood panels before the couch, where he was bent over to rest on the pillows, as she understood his actions.

Bridget was sure John had known she was there. After all, she'd stopped twice to trumpet her arrival with a series of loud meows, since the giants seemed to respond more to that sound than they did her hair or tail signals. But he had offered no acknowledging signs in return, choosing instead to eye a bundle of glossy compressed deadwood leaves in his lap. That in itself no longer offended the kitten; under Jessica's constant love, Bridget had decided to ignore these insults from John – especially since he was so hard to read, with so much of his hairless body concealed within those dry artificial skins. But the minute Bridget had leapt high onto the deadwood hall trim, sinking her claws in to climb after that hazelnut moth clinging to the ceiling, the John giant had erupted into a volcanic rage! Bridget had just waited there, curling her spine and rolling her ears to show her purpose. Can't you see that taunting moth? Its extra eyes shuttering open and closed with each twitch of its wings? But John hadn't cared. Screaming out in anger, he'd tossed aside his all-important paper bundle to scramble to his feet, only to think better of it and pick back up the glossy papers, rolling them into a rod that his giant hands waved like a mace. Since Bridget had learned early on what sort of blows John could give with rolled paper leaves, she'd left the aggravating moth and fled for sanctuary under Jessica's dress skirts.

There were many things about that incident Bridget still didn't understand. Chief among them: why the John giant would let a dirty old moth hang wherever it pleased, and yet Bridget had to stay off just about everything but the deadwood beneath them.

It helped that the John bull just disappeared during most of the daylight. It was a curious action, suggesting he might be any one of all sorts of mystical

nightmarish creatures that those other fellows in the old giant's world had whispered about when they were all curled together trying to get some sleep. But Bridget discounted such things, since the lady Jessica certainly liked curling up with him, and she seemed an ordinary enough giant, even if she did have some hair. So Bridget used his absences to hang onto Jessica's neck, curl in her lap, or just follow her around. The love aura surrounding the female giant was intoxicating! But when the lady giant was too active, or herself seemed to disappear, Bridget would find a spot in the sun and ponder all the mysteries of her new home – like the enormous transparent walls. True, it was sometimes difficult finding spots to gaze through that were clear of skin oils, smoke smears, dust beds, spider webs, and random hair nests, but when she did, Bridget could look upon a world both altogether new and strangely familiar. As much as she enjoyed prancing atop the tables, knocking off the knick-knacks, and sliding across the kitchen counters, often she found contentment just staring out those windows and dreaming of chasing the bounding robins, shredding the tulips, or investigating the high oak's nests.

It was in the midst of such a dream that she met Scarface, and learned the sorrows of temptation.

Of course, we shouldn't get too far ahead of ourselves in this tale. For the path to Scarface leads first through another.

Nine

Nighttime always fascinated Bridget – so much so that she often napped during the afternoon, assuring her plenty of time to explore the darkness. It was as if the world itself changed when the sun took to its rest, mutating from something that made perfect sense to one's eyes, ears, and nose – an environment of majesty, seeped in His beauty – to become an all-surrounding mystery, dampening all perceptions, encroaching upon rationality, where even the truths before you became uncertain.

Nothing could better suit a creature driven by curiosity.

Bridget didn't give in to it at once, of course. She started each night with John and Jessica, watching them cuddle on their big padded board, listening to their pitter patter. While that itself could be fun, it was but the opening act. When all was said and done, Jessica would often end up curled into a ball, her head nestled against her pillow or John's strong left arm, her knees rolled beneath her chin, her lips ever smiling. Often that's how she would awaken with the dawn.

John, on the other hand, was much more mobile. Starting with his arms about his wife, the bull would soon roll onto his back. His nose would wiggle as if to dislodge a mosquito. He'd snort, and then his hips would shudder. With sluggish twists he'd adjust his back and legs so that they'd churn like the waves on Bridget's water dish, his nose honking all the while in short, hoggish snorts. His head would shake, bobbing against the pillows as his spine relaxed. And then, when he was at peace in his dreams, would come the snoring.

The first time she'd heard that low, vibrating crescendo, not unlike a foghorn being dragged over a washboard, Bridget had almost fallen off the refrigerator in complete and utter shock. She'd never imagined such an ominous combination of shattering and shrieking sensations – and yet she didn't fear it. It seemed like part of the darkness, at home in the mystery. So, once she'd calmed herself, she'd released the cricket and came running to see what this new element was, or if something was dying. Thus it saddened her to discover this noise was only the bumbling breathing of the humorless giant. Still, it was such a quirky sound, a mischievous achievement that she wouldn't have expected from the hard one, that Bridget forever changed her night exploring habits to enjoy it.

Sometimes she'd just sit there, listening to his mouth pipes all night. Sometimes she wouldn't. After all, around the house there were crickets chirping, roaches marching, moths fluttering, locusts buzzing, bats sounding, hellhounds howling, mice scurrying, air vents blowing, curtains billowing, moonbeams flirting, floorboards creaking, old walls groaning – and all of it in complete darkness.

What cat could resist that?

There were times Bridget wanted to. Times when the cold settled in, and nestling against Jessica's neck seemed like heaven. Or when John got boisterous in his soundings, and his mouth opened so wide, Bridget could gaze in to see the little pink digit dancing in the caverns of his throat. Many a night she'd sit at attention at his chin, stabbing with her left paw at the throbbing stalactite, but it always seemed to evade her touch. Other times Bridget would stick her nose into

his mouth, trying to get a better view of how that thing moved so. Once she managed to get her whole spotted head snuggled in there, only to find there wasn't room for a paw. Then came the hot, damp bellows. To her fortune, she'd clamped shut her ears before that, or else the resounding thunder might have sent her scurrying down his chest with her claws in full glory. As it was, his moist breath permeated her fur like a thick fog, so that as she squeezed her head out, the hair about her neck and chin hung limp and soggy, like bits of Jessica's alleged cat food after it had floated awhile in her water dish.

Jessica rose the next morning to find John hanging over the bathroom sink, sucking up handfuls of water, only to spit them out.

"Hi, honey," she'd mumbled, hugging him. "Something wrong?"

"I've got a mouthful of fur," he grumbled.

Jessica managed a weary smile as she walked back out of the bathroom to the kitchen. "I know just how you feel," she said.

John stopped, surprised. "No – I mean it. I've really got a mouth full of fur."

"Sure you do, honey."

And so it went.

As the novelty of John's window-rattling snores wore down, and the little pink digit seemed ever more elusive, Bridget started leaving them as the music began, returning her night eyes to the mysteries about her. The crickets that seemed to know every crack in every wall, the colonies of crawling bugs that nestled under the cabinets, the footprints of the mice – that sort of thing. The most fun escapades, though, were the ones that brought discovery.

One night she was playing with a little black spider she'd found on the big pillowy lounger. She was chasing the critter, letting it escape, then pinning it back down again, when during one flight the tiny bug scrambled beneath John's favorite little box. Bridget sprang on the hard, bumpy thing, thinking it'd give her eight-legged toy a good jolt. Just then a surprise burst echoed from the wall. Bridget leapt to the top of the lounger's padded ledge; the favorite little box, meanwhile, slid off its pillowed arm. Across the way, the black picture window beside the bookshelf started glowing, even as a series of crashes and rat-a-tat impacts seemed to come from its insides.

Bridget almost jumped with joy. She just loved that magical thing!

The picture window had a large square top of polished artificial wood – you know, the kind that looked like all that smooth, dark deadwood the giants loved around their house, but stank of old oil and had little more thickness than one of John's artificial skins. When the picture window was "awake," or in other words, when it was actually showing moving images of things across time and space, that shiny artificial top would get nice and warm. The few times Bridget had been there, it had seemed more appealing than the sunny windowsill! But for some reason John never wanted her lying atop his picture window; indeed, he had always reserved some of his angriest assaults for when she tried. She had never understood that – and now was her chance to figure out why!

With three bounds Bridget was lying in comfort on the active box, which was now filling the dark room with dancing gray ghosts and a stream of high-charged echoes, shouts and screams and explosions and concussions and who knows what else. None of that mattered to the spotted kitten. She sprawled her growing body across the smooth surface and waited for it to warm up.

Then Bridget heard random flex twangs from the soft board beneath her sleeping giants. Suspecting their rise, she fled into the dining room shadows.

"What is it?" came Jessica's weary voice.

"Don't know," John mumbled, his ragged gait carrying his half-asleep body up to the picture window. Smacking his dry lips, the giant turned his head one way, then the other. When that brought no answers, Bridget watched his chin drop so that he could view his beloved window. "TV came on somehow, I guess. War picture."

"Well turn it off and come to bed," Jessica called.

John mumbled his agreement. Taking one last look around, he stumbled over to the beaten couch and bent to retrieve his favorite box.

Just like that, the picture window went dead.

Bridget half-expected him to take the box back to Jessica, but he only scratched his nose, leaving the remote on the cushy arm.

Something about that intrigued Bridget. Without waiting for the spider to return, she scampered across the floorboards and leaped atop the box.

The picture window crackled back to life!

"John," came Jessica's tired voice, "you forgot to turn it off."

Bridget started to hide as the pale gray light illuminated her, but then she realized she didn't need to.

"Get up, John! You left the TV on!"

"Ah, honey, are you sure?"

A cavalcade of roaring tempests shook the picture window, the floor, the transparent wall – just about everything.

Bridget heard Jessica's head snap up on their padded night board. "Don't you go back to sleep, John Michael Fergus – "

"All right," he interrupted her.

But Jessica wasn't finished. "Go turn that off! Now!"

Bridget recognized that tone – and so she hid, all the while priding herself on a fantastic discovery. Not only had she figured out what fed the window, but more important, she knew now how to get that John giant up in the middle of the night!

You see, for a while now she'd been thinking of different things she could do to him. Not that she disliked him; he was mated to Jessica, after all, so Bridget felt obligated to like him. But the more she was around the bull giant, the more Bridget couldn't help thinking that he just wasn't very nice. No, that wasn't the right word – he was quite loving to Jessica, and so he had to be a gentle, protective, compassionate giant. He just wasn't kind to *her*. More important, Bridget thought John wasn't responding well to her training. For example, Jessica was learning how and when Bridget wanted fed, her sandbox replaced, her water changed, her back rubbed, her sleep undisturbed... all that sort of thing. But John was a different story.

The great test came a couple of nights later. Bridget had been stalking a moonbeam that kept floating across the floor – it was just a fun sort of game to her – when she spied something fluttering atop the bookshelf. At first, it made no sense; she knew there weren't any birds in there! And indeed, when she stopped to stare up at the high edge, remaining frozen for who knows how long, nothing happened. But then the breeze came out of the floor vent, and there, at the edge of the bookshelf, Bridget saw it. The unmistakable waving of feathered wings!

Now, you must understand that not even Jessica liked Bridget climbing the bookshelf, as the kitten well knew. Every time Bridget had tried, Jessica had shooed her away, her touch gentle yet firm, saying something about how she had to take care around Sebastian, whoever he was. And since Bridget loved Jessica, she felt it necessary to try to accommodate the gentle giant on things like the bookshelf, especially since Jessica was responding so well to her training.

But on the other hand, Bridget knew Jessica wouldn't want any birds or bats, rats, or ostriches in the house. Probably not any snakes, lizards, pigs, or goats, either. And heaven forbid, not a dog! If she ever saw any of them around, Bridget

felt it was her responsibility to get rid of them as quickly as possible – even if it meant climbing the bookshelf.

So up she went.

Ten

The bookshelves sat atop a hollow cliff of polished deadwood. Bridget soared to its top and immediately knocked over something cold and shiny. It fell with a crash. Startled, Bridget fled behind the pillowy furniture thing.

As she settled into the shadows, she heard the mumbled words she'd known would follow.

"What was that, John? John? *John!* Oh, wake up, John! How can you sleep at a time like this?"

"When else should I sleep, dear?"

A loud thump answered him, followed by a groan. After a few deep breaths, his broad feet started staggering across the deadwood planks, heading toward the disturbance, which this time was the bookshelf.

"Looks like a picture frame broke, honey."

"How did that happen?"

"I don't know. Maybe the cat got it."

"She doesn't jump up there, dear. I've trained her."

"Right."

And so he stumbled back to the padded board. Bridget just sat there, thinking. She'd always just assumed the stuff above the cliff was like the stuff inside the cliff. She'd snuck in there once when Jessica had one of its wooden walls pulled away. The innards were shaped like the bookshelves above, layered deadwood planks stacked with dusty, forgotten things Jessica kept there – odd boxes filled with bound paper leaves and rattling articles, strange flat squares, and soft, flimsy items. It made a comfortable nesting place, Bridget decided, and became quite fun when the feminine giant had closed the wall on her. But outside of some holes to hide in, the innards soon lost their appeal. The mice hadn't found it yet, so it housed little but spiders. That made it quite lonely.

None of that mattered now, of course, but it was the kind of dead-end thinking that Bridget often experienced. After all, she was a cat.

The truth was, she really didn't know too much about those bookshelves, but that didn't matter because the bird was still up there, taunting her every time the air blew. So Bridget curled her tail tight and leaped for the clifftop. Once again she collided with something. But rather than hide, the kitten jumped for what looked like a hole on the second shelf. Even as she heard Jessica moan – "There it is again, John. John? John!" – Bridget slid into something startling: another cat.

He was like nothing she'd ever seen before. Less than half her size, this newcomer sat upright on his paws in a self-assured greeting. His tail curled about his feet, making no resistance. His fur lay smooth against his skin, promising peace and contentment. His eyes were broad and moist, offering friendship. And he made no sound, guaranteeing Bridget self-determination.

All this made her tingle with excitement, and yet there was something distinctly odd about this cat. His fur was of the purest white – but for an unusual smattering of dust, of all things – and the flow of it shimmered smooth and bright, just like the surface of the transparent walls. His movement, if indeed this cat did move, was as slow as the sun. And strangest of all, he had no odor. None at all.

Confused, Bridget sent him all sorts of signals. He returned not one. His welcoming messages remained unbroken. His eyes sparkled, as blinding white as his fur.

"OK, honey," came John's reluctant voice.

Not knowing what to do, Bridget touched noses with the newcomer. His was cold, and seemed wet. That made her fearful for his health, but the groaning floorboard spurred her to rush, and so she leaped for the top shelf. Since it was as wide as the middle one, she had to grab hold of its side and pull herself up. She only hoped John didn't see her, but that fear soon was forgotten. For there, before her, was the bird!

It was a long, straight thing, with thin feathers that billowed up with the breeze. It stank of old, clinging dirt. But that didn't matter, did it? Bridget didn't think so. All birds stank, didn't they? So Bridget threw herself at it, her paws crushing down whole layers of feathers to a single thin bone. That made no sense, so Bridget pawed the creature, again and again, each time finding nothing there but hairlike, dusty feathers latched to a single, lifeless limb.

The wood planks creaked. On instinct Bridget kicked the bird off, giving it a chance to flee. Instead, it plunged over the side. Bridget started to follow it, then crept back into the darkness. John was there!

"Looks like another picture frame, dear," he mumbled.

"What caused that?"

"How should I know? No – wait a minute. You're dust bunny's here."

"My what?"

"Your dust bunny. You know; that fluffy rainbow wand you use to dust things with when you're in too big a hurry to do a good job."

"Oh, funnnnnny. I wouldn't be in such a hurry to come back to bed if I were you!"

John chuckled. Bridget saw him pick up the bird, waving it before his head.

"You know, this thing doesn't look too used – YEOW!"

"John?" Jessica cried out. "What's wrong, John?"

"Oh, it's that crazy cat of yours!"

For the rest of her life, Bridget could never recall just what had made her attack like that. Perhaps it was the way the light flittered through the waving feathers, or how John's hand had rocked the bird back and forth, or maybe the inner joy she knew she'd feel if just once she'd given that brash bull what he deserved. Whatever her motivation, it had sent her plunging down from the top shelf to sink her claws into John's shoulder. When he screamed, she'd latched her front paws into the bird and slapped it forward – which just happened to end up inside John's bellowing mouth. So she'd leaped up, landing thick in the hairy crown atop his head, only to realize that wasn't really a great place to be, so she skipped down to his other shoulder and into the shadows at his feet. Those she kicked, just for good measure.

John yelled again. "BRIDGET! Where is that darn cat!?!"

Thrilled beyond care, Bridget clung to the shadows at the foot of the cliff. John hopped around, rubbing his feet where she'd nailed them. Once, twice, three times he'd stared right into her hiding spot, but never did he react. So she took a chance, diving out to spear his toes, then scoot back behind the corner. He squealed, spinning to the attack. But he wasn't fast enough to see her.

"You blasted cat! Where are you?"

Jessica started laughing.

"BRIDGET!" he snapped. "I'm going to – YEOW!"

That one he'd done on his own. Stomping in a dark circle, John rammed his left

foot into the sleeping picture window. Bridget just stood in the shadows, enjoying the best discovery of her career. These slow giants just didn't stand a chance of catching her in the darkness!

That got her to wondering if anything could – come sun or moon.

"Oh, honey," giggled Jessica, "you'd better just come to bed."

"Oh no! I'm not going to let that – YEOW!"

Pulling away from his heels, Bridget took pride in herding the bull back to his padded board. From that point on, she knew things would be different. Her giants might claim the day, but she owned the night!

Eleven

One afternoon Bridget was awakened from her nap by a shrill, yet somewhat muffled scratching. But as she stretched against the bare windowsill, basking in the warm rays of the sun, she was too contented to bother getting up. So Bridget raised an eyelid, saw nothing going on, and went back to sleep. Or she would have, if the scratching hadn't returned at twice its earlier pace. This time she raised her head, circling her eyes about to see what it was.

What she found made Bridget forget all about sleeping.

Sitting atop the peeling wood planks on the other side of the transparent wall was a large cat. At first glance he seemed appealing to Bridget, his frame tall and lean, his long, matted coat a patchwork of grays and black streaks on a hazel background. He sat upright, showing respect, but his tail whipped itself from side to side, signaling impatience. His fur twitched along his spine – another message of frustration – but his eyes and ears both spread wide towards Bridget, showing the newcomer valued what she had to say. Yet that didn't last. Soon his lime green eyes squinted inward, as an accusation or judgment.

That drew out the scar along his left cheek, an old wound long since healed, though it had left a jagged patch of bare pink skin from his lips to his neck. Bridget then saw that wasn't his only mark – something had carved a slice from his right ear. The sight brought her pain. She winced, which made him smile.

Bridget started to crawl back from the windowsill, only to stop out of stubbornness. What reason did she have to fear him? Even if he meant harm, the shiny wall stood

between them!

Not that he could hurt her, in any case – or so she thought.

He rolled his head back and laughed.

"What makes you think I want trouble?" he called through the wall.

At first, Bridget couldn't understand what he said. That aggravated him. His tail smacked into the deadwood with a loud flap.

"If I wanted trouble, I'd not have scratched the glass," he said, his eyes glaring hot. "I'd have rammed it hard. Scared you good."

Bridget found herself stumbling over some of his words. He chuckled at her ignorance.

"No, little one," he told her, "I was simply wondering who'd replaced Sebastian in this prison."

"Sebastian?" Bridget felt a sudden thrill. Pointing to the bookshelf, she called, "You mean him? Up there?"

That brought more snickering. The newcomer's ears flattened, showing contempt.

"Sebastian," he told her, "was the old warrior who guarded this lady before you got here. A worthy cat, that one." Then his tone hardened. "I was his next in line."

Bridget didn't know what that meant. Sure, she'd found some old fur lying around, and smelled the presence of others before her, but every place she'd ever been had such things. Not that this interloper cared, of course. He read the confusion in her eyes, her tail, and answered with open boredom. His head drooped, then turned away.

"Wait!" she called. "I'm a good warrior!"

"You?" That drew his haunting eyes back, if only to scoff at her. "You're barely old enough to draw your claws."

Bridget didn't understand what he was talking about, but the prideful way he said it made her envious. Now she wanted to be a warrior! The very best warrior!

"I can so!" she declared. "I got the John giant! I made him run! Several times!"

"So what? He's a buffoon!"

Bridget added that to the list of words she needed to learn. But she didn't have to know what it meant to feel defensive about it. His tone made that plain.

"But he's all I've got!" she wailed.

"In there, maybe. But you don't have to stay in that prison."

Bridget sat down, drawing her tail about her. "What prison?"

The newcomer leaned back and laughed.

"You mean here?" she pondered. This place wasn't a prison! That metal string cage she'd been trapped in, or that box – those were prisons. Not Jessica's home!

He laughed even harder.

"But I can go anywhere I want!" she protested.

"Anywhere?"

He slapped his right paw against the clear wall. Bridget leaped back in surprise. "Then come out here," he demanded. "With me."

Ever since she'd felt Jessica's love, Bridget had never thought much about doing that. She'd dreamed about it, but never more than that. There was no need. She had everything she wanted right here! But now, with his taunting, it no longer seemed enough.

"Can you climb these trees?" he said. "Chase through the grass? Run down the butterflies? The birds? No, you can't do any of that. You're locked within that little house. Trapped. Never to feel the earth between your pads, the summer wind blowing warm across your spine."

He rose, stretching his front legs, his back. With a pitiful shrug, he turned away, leaving Bridget feeling lost and hopeless as he sauntered across the porch's old wood planks for the trees beyond. But at the splintery edge, just before he jumped away, the battle-hardened feline turned back. His eyes were as hot coals.

"And you call yourself a warrior," he spat. "You're nothing."

Twelve

Things were never the same after that. Bridget had uncorked an envious specter in her heart, and it started to consume her.

Be content with this little house? With these few filtered rays of sun? With this boring food, artificial furniture, and deadwood surroundings? With these unimaginative giants and their controlled, one-sided affections?

And you call yourself a warrior. You're NOTHING.

Don't think Bridget buckled under such attacks from their start. Far from it. At first, she found it easy to keep a proper perspective. Though she didn't realize it, Bridget was maturing both in body and mind. She understood more of the world around her. She saw the dangers in jealousy and discontent. And Jessica never hid her undemanding love. In her beloved's shining presence, that truth shredded all doubts. But when Bridget was alone, temptation gnawed at her – little by little, with ever sharper teeth.

As the fall settled in, and Jessica's studies resumed, Bridget found her favorite giant disappearing more and more. One day Bridget saw how it happened, via a massive rectangular hole in the wall. She couldn't believe it – Jessica was leaving

the house! That rocked the growing cat. To think that her Jessica and John had moving walls just like the older, hound-loving giant had!

It was so simple, Bridget had to wonder why she'd never realized it before. But of course, deep down, she knew the answer to that one. Scarface had said it, more or less – in her overwhelming joy, Bridget had blinded herself to what was going on around her. All this time John had been leaving by day, and she'd never caught on. He'd been coming back at nightfall, and she'd never figured it out. Not even when Jessica did it, as Bridget knew she had.

That knowledge created a wound inside Bridget. She didn't know what to do about the weight on her heart, so she turned to Jessica, curling up to her whenever she could, following her every step, meowing in longing for her attention and purring her thanks at the least bit of affection.

Jessica tried to accommodate her beloved cat, for she recognized something was amiss and wanted to help. But time was quite precious now. Jessica's class work had started anew, putting a heavy burden on her mind, and of course, the household chores remained ever steady. So in the end, Jessica found herself setting Bridget aside more and more – which only made the young cat hurt even more.

The wall holes began to fascinate the cat. Whatever was beyond these things occupied both of her giants, so it only made sense that if Bridget found a way to get out, she could follow them. She could share what they did, and she could escape the great limitation this house put upon her. She would no longer be a prisoner.

Freedom... it had called to her ever since she'd been dumped into that paper sack, which was as far back as Bridget could remember. Now she was determined to win her liberty!

But how?

Day after day, night after night, Bridget went over the possibilities. Many a time she thought she'd worked out a plan, only for it to unravel on some small detail. Then one plot worked to perfection. Seeing John off in the morning, Jessica stayed by the swinging wall to chat with him of beloved things, and so doing, she kept the portal wedged open. Bridget had only to slip by her feet to the great beyond! So she crept up to her giant's bare toes. There she paused to bask in the fresh, grassy air, which was only a bit tainted by the scent of Jessica's bare soles. She heard the echoes of Scarface's harsh voice calling to her, beckoning her on, even as

the urge to bound away gripped her from her shoulders to her paws. And yet Jessica's voice was there, full of grace and hope and beauty, and the young cat felt a chilling emptiness just thinking about leaving. So she didn't.

That brought some satisfaction, but it also raised the volume on the Scarface memories. Bridget began to hate the dim shadows, for in each layer of twilight she saw that tempter's face, and heard his accusations.

You're nothing. You're NOTHING. YOU'RE NOTHING NOTHING NOTHING!

Now all pleasures turned perverse. Bridget no longer found joy in sliding across the kitchen counters or attacking the wavy curtains. Tossing the pillows only aggravated her. Even taunting John had no flavor.

It all came to a boil with one full moon. Bridget sat on a pile of artificial skins atop Jessica's dusty deadwood drawers, watching her beloved giant fall asleep in John's cherished arms. Bridget waited, and waited, and waited. But for some reason, John seemed content on holding his mate. He wasn't rolling about and snorting out his usual thunderous racket!

Bridget couldn't believe it. Here it was, near the peak of blackness, and she'd wasted it waiting for the opening notes of his blow-horn pipes that he'd decided not to play!

How could things possibly get worse?!?

In frustration, Bridget kicked off some boxes and things that John liked to unload atop the drawers for some unthinkable reason. They landed with a muffled groan on the deadwood planks.

Jessica snapped alert, going in an instant from a restful sleep to an upright, timid cringing. Bridget enjoyed seeing that whenever it happened, though it was small consolation now.

"John!" the beloved giant whispered. "John!"

He smiled in his sleep, nudging closer to her.

"Not now, John! Wake up! Someone's on the porch!"

That drew a moan, but little else, so Jessica jabbed his gut with her elbow. He groaned much louder that time.

"Come on, honey!" she urged. "Wake up! I heard someone on the porch!"

Bridget didn't know what to do. This should have cheered her up. The silly things Jessica often asked John to do usually set him up as Bridget's plaything. But the developing feline didn't feel like herding him tonight.

She couldn't help noticing that John might be figuring this out. "Ah, dear, it's probably just the cat."

That heightened Bridget's frustration. That's all she was – "just the cat." She didn't know just what that meant, but the droll feelings he placed on the words were unmistakable.

Torn by indecision, Bridget stretched her arms and legs. Her left paw pushed aside a set of bound metal pieces. They fell with a dull thud.

"You hear that?" Jessica snapped, only to muffle her voice. "There's something at the door! They have keys!"

"Oh, think about it! Why would a burglar try a set of keys on our door?"

"What's he going to use – ear swabs? How should I know?"

"Exactly."

"Oh, you John Michael Ferguson you! Go check that porch!"

"Dear, I think that came from in here."

"No, it wasn't!"

"Probably that cat," continued John, glancing about the shadows.

"Just go check the porch, honey! Please?"

Bridget had long ago learned that all Jessica had to do to get her way was to say "Please?" in that sweet, subtle, seductive way of hers. It didn't work when Bridget tried that. She could never quite get the sound right – and besides, she had difficulties grasping subtlety.

With a little hesitation and some grousing, John dragged on his robe, rammed his feet into his slippers, and shoved them through the hall to the front room – keeping a careful eye all the while for any sign that sly cat was on the prowl. That gave Bridget some comfort, and yet she still felt a restless anger inside.

That's one reason why she charged.

Like most of God's great mysteries, it happened before Bridget ever realized it could happen. John turned the grinding metal bits that allowed the swinging wall to open – but instead of going outside, he just stood there, holding the wall ajar with his arm. That was her opportunity. Bridget took one look at the cloaking darkness beyond the deadwood and ran past him. Even as John called out in distress, a cold, wet breeze refreshed and fulfilled her. She leaped off the outside paint-chipped planks into long, vibrant grass up to her ears, and felt God's own soil beneath her pads. A peaty aroma enveloped her. Invigorated in a way she'd not felt before, as if she was experiencing God's creation for the first time, Bridget charged helter-skelter through the dark. The tall elm reared before her. Dashing up Sebastian's grave, she threw herself against that proud tree as high as she could and dug her claws into its thick trunk.

Hanging there drove every trace of anguish from her soul.

At long last, she was free!

Thirteen

The old deadwood groaned once, twice. Bridget turned an ear, recognizing the sound, even though she'd never heard such impact stresses happen so quickly together. Then came an awkward, flopping plop on the grassy earth. "Bridget!" came John's bellow. "Stay!"

Even if she'd known what that meant, Bridget wouldn't have listened. Fearing John intended to punish her, which was probably a good bet, Bridget threw herself into the darkness beyond the elm – a place she'd never seen even from the windowsill. She ran into thick, damp air and tall grass, seeing little around her and recognizing even less. John's footfalls pounded in her wake.

"Bridget!" he shouted. Curious… she heard desperation in his words, even fear. "Bridget, don't go! Please, Bridget. BRIDGET!"

She continued on, losing all sense of him in the thicket. Her long, graceful bounds carried her high over a shallow stone ramp into a barren flatland. The dry earth scraped against her pads. She stopped to lick them, hating the ashen taste, only to forget all about that in a fearful gaze at the dead zone surrounding her. Straight and true it flowed, this somewhat soft, black rock that she sat on, and yet it glowed in the dim white light that groped its way through air so wet, it seemed to float around Bridget like the very breath of God. The dead zone ran to either side as a long, unbroken path of streaked jet, fading only within the dark of night and the slow, rolling mist.

Bridget sat in the shallow abyss, marveling at the almost smooth rock, the thick fog. That zone amplified the undercurrent of chirps and buzzes, distant barks and shrill calls. This was the world she'd long dreamed of, the land of warriors. This was where she belonged!

Then she spied the twin jewels sparkling through the night.

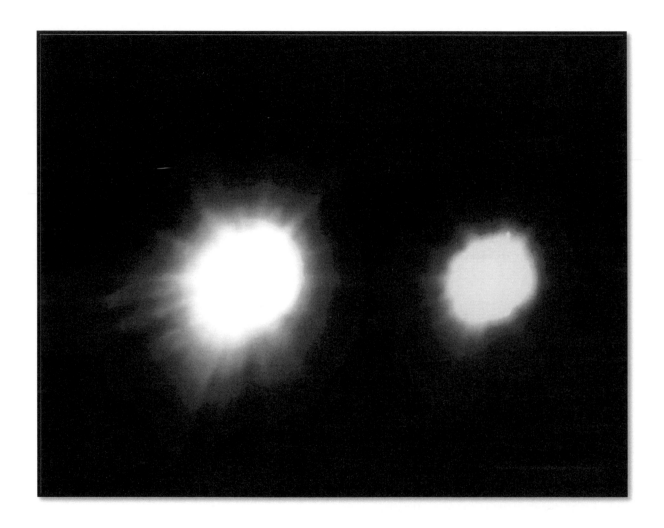

"So beautiful," Bridget whispered. They fascinated her, beckoning her to sit and partake of their magnificence, and yet she had no time to study them, for with each breath these twin orbs grew larger, piercing the mist. Bridget felt their presence in the rock – a low, emerging rumble. The two small suns approached, their light filling the fog, and then like a storm they rolled forth, flooding her ears with thunder.

"Run!" came a brash order. "Get out of there!"

Bridget didn't heed that. She felt entranced by the brilliant blindness. If she only held her ground, she knew the onrushing stars would soon be upon her. What a glorious experience that would be!

A tiny shadow fell around Bridget, like a black spot against the overwhelming light. Something shoved her into the hard curb. At once the twin jewels swept by, followed by a hot rush of pummeling turbulence. She cowered in the shoulder of the rock, fearing the passing of doom.

But then, just as quick as it had come, the enigma was gone. Bridget was alone in the mist.

No, not alone, she realized. Scarface stood beside her, scowling.

"What were you trying to do?" the old veteran scolded. "Get us both killed?"

"Killed?" Bridget repeated, denoting another word to learn.

Scarface crawled atop the small ledge of rock. "First things first. Never, and I mean NEVER, look into the eyes of a dragon. They'll just squash you flat. Don't attack them, don't try to outrun them, and don't try to climb on them. And for goodness sake, don't crawl into their mouths when they sleep. I know it's warm in there, but you can't ever take their silence for granted. They come alive as fast as lightning, and then they'll just chew you up and spit you out, so don't do it."

Still petrified by the rushing thunder, Bridget shook her head in quaking obedience. The old tabby looked down upon her and mellowed.

"Oh, don't be so scared. They're not so hard to escape. Look at you; you're still here, aren't you? And I'll tell you a little secret – they're not as tough as they seem. Look at me!" Scarface stressed, rolling his tail through the hole in his right ear. "One cold night I crawled deep inside one's mouth, and all it could get the next morning was this!"

Bridget sat up, finding little reassurance in the old cat's words.

"But I thought, I mean, I thought you got that from being a warrior."

Scarface leaned back and laughed, flapping the tall grass with his tail. "No,

squirt, no, though that's what others think. I let them; it makes them respect me more." Then he tapped the crease in his face with his left paw. "But this one, it was from fighting – and that's just the start. I've got many others."

To be honest, Bridget didn't like looking at that scar now any more than she had before. Yet something about it gave her a perverse thrill.

"That must have hurt," she offered as bait, hoping he'd talk about it.

"Of course! But it's nothing you'd want, squirt. The best warriors, they find ways to escape these things. Like Sebastian. But sometimes it's got to be done. I had to take this one. If I hadn't, that old boxer hound would've bitten Sebastian good. I had to take it, for him."

Bridget felt a burden on her heart. "You mean, like you just did here, for me."

Scarface's eyes narrowed, burning in the dim light.

"Don't you think I'll always be there. A good warrior doesn't rely on others to bail him out. He's strong! He's resourceful! He's independent! And," Scarface added, almost as an afterthought, "he looks out for others. Before himself, if need be."

With a deep breath, he flexed his strong muscles, rippling his matted calico fur from his ears to his tail. Then he rose, stretched again, and glared down at Bridget with a defiant, almost mischievous smile.

"But he always survives," the tabby stressed. "He perseveres – over everything else. He triumphs. Remember that."

Fourteen

"Well, don't just sit there," Scarface growled. "Get out of that street! We've got to get you home."

Bridget stretched her muscles, which were still sore with tension fatigue, and skipped to the top of the curb. Scarface's belittling bothered her, though she would never have admitted that, such was her admiration and respect for his feats. He had turned his back to Bridget as he rambled into a line of unkempt brush, so she pushed herself after him.

"Hey now, squirt," he called as he passed into deep shadows within a line of spreading oaks. "What are you doing out here, anyway?"

Bridget struggled to keep pace. He moved so fast!

"I wanted out," she answered between bounds. "They couldn't... they couldn't stop me!"

As that rolled off her tongue, the cats moved beyond the street lamps into a worn field of weed patches and damp, moldy earth. The crystalline fog, which she had first found so beautiful, now blended with the night to hide most everything – including Scarface. Fearful, Bridget slowed in a sand pool amidst the trees, barely able to see even her own paws. Something hooted high among the fluttering leaves. She cringed.

At once Scarface was there, standing above her, chuckling. "Come along, little warrior. We'll get you home."

He disappeared with a silent leap. Embarrassed at being left behind, Bridget charged into the mist, racing to catch the ghostly image of his tail. Branches and weed stalks flew by, but she seemed unable to gain any ground. Each time she increased her speed he did as well, with far greater ease. The effort soon had her legs aching and her pads sore, with thorns snagging her fur, but Bridget pushed on. Her nose started to run from the heat of her exertions, even as her throat throbbed against the chill, wet air.

Step by step Scarface pulled ever ahead. To Bridget, he was like a wraith – appearing for a moment before her, then fading within the dark. More and more Bridget had to follow his scent, but soon that too disappeared, as did his tracks. So she slowed to rest, though it galled her to do it, and tried to figure out where Scarface had gone. That led her to a far more discouraging problem: Bridget had no idea where she was or what she was doing.

"Oh, stop fretting so!" Scarface whispered. "You think this will change things?"

Shocked and humiliated by his sudden appearance, Bridget nearly raked his face with her claws. How did he keep sneaking up on her?

She could see his amusement in his glowing eyes, but he made no sport of it. "We mustn't stop here," Scarface warned. "The hounds patrol this place all the time. Come on now! Follow me! We're almost there."

With that, he was off once more. Bridget swallowed her pride and shoved her weary self forward. But this time Scarface moved ahead at a slow clip to help her keep pace. Beneath a thick shrub he came to rest alongside a wall of gray deadwood planks, slivered and cracked from decay. Bridget rolled to a stop at his feet, gasping.

"So, you wanted to be a warrior," he reminded her. "Well here's your chance. We've got to cross under this fence to get you home. You must be swift and silent, or the hounds will get us both. So stay close, squirt! I don't want to have to save you again."

Bridget offered a timid nod. She saw his tense muscles, calculating eyes, and flattened hair. It gave her courage.

Without another word, Scarface crawled into an eroded hole in the dirt that stretched below the bug-gnarled boards. Flattening his back, the large cat scooted under the fence with little difficulty. He waited on the other side for Bridget to come through, and then he bounded into a black forest. She followed, focusing on his darting tail. All she wanted was to escape this place. The scent of dog corrupted the sod, the grass, the air itself. It maddened her.

A barricade of dense brush rose before Scarface. It brought Bridget some joy, for upon its damp leaves and fallen needles sparkled the light of the pale midnight sun. The male warrior paid it no heed, springing through the branches to splatter Bridget with dew drops. Blinded, she plunged after him. On the other side she sensed a clearing. She sprinted ahead, batting her eyes clear, then froze.

Bridget stood at the center of a grassy knoll, far from the circling tree line. Scarface was gone, but she wasn't alone. Poised at the foot of the hill stood a mountainous German Shepherd, her sharp black eyes targeting Bridget with dark, restless malice.

"Scarface!" Bridget cried out.

A cross bark answered from behind the cat, followed by a second and third. The hound at Bridget's face snarled, then charged.

Fifteen

Instinct drove Bridget straight into the sprinting hound. After all, that's how she'd always handled the other fellows who'd attacked her – and it had always worked. Even with John.

So, no one was more surprised than Bridget when the German Shepherd met her assault head-on. Bridget snarled. She flung herself at the black and brown snout, her claws exposed, her budding fangs cutting the breeze. The shepherd answered by sitting down. As Bridget dove for her throat, the dog lifted a paw and swatted the errant cat away as she might a pesky fly.

An avalanche of barks descended upon Bridget. Aggravated into a mad frenzy, she threw herself back at the giant hound. The dog brushed her aside, sending her rolling like a tumbleweed. Bridget bounded back, dodging this way and that to confuse the dog and shake her pursuers. The shepherd watched all this with impassive eyes. When Bridget struck, the dog knocked her down once more – and held her there.

Bridget didn't know what to make of all this. Three times she'd stalked this terror, only to be deflected with no more effort than the young cat might have handled the pillows in Jessica's house! And now Bridget was pinned against the earth by an overpowering paw planted right between her shoulders! Try as she might, Bridget couldn't squeeze from under it. She was trapped!

Into that frightening thought broke a chorus of barks and yips. From around the trees they came, pounding upon the cat's ears with horrid ferocity. That recharged Bridget. With new vigor, she struggled against the paw, crazed by the barks and what they foretold, but to no avail. She couldn't get out. The crescendo heightened. Bridget shuttered her eyes, not wanting to see the end.

She heard a stampede of reckless feet around her. She felt bursts of hot breath. *This is it*, she knew. *It's all over.*

A small, wet nose pushed into her backside. Thick, dripping tongues invaded her ears, even as a miniature mouth nipped her snout. Dog drool pooled on her paws.

In humiliation, Bridget wanted to cry out to God. *Help me, Lord! It's a swarm of puppies!*

She tried to swat at them, but with their mom holding her down, the five little shepherds had no trouble evading her. So Bridget had to lay there, submitting to their gentle washing, pawing, and teasing. All the while she kept asking herself, *So where's the great warrior? Where's this great ruler of the dark?*

"Scarface was right," she mumbled. "I'm nothing."

With a chill growl, everything changed. Bridget heard it just as soon as did the puppies – a thick, trembling pulsation of pure terror. The little dogs fled before the

growl. Even the mother bowed to it.

As Bridget felt the weighty paw slip from her back, she sensed a horrible shadow draw near. It filled her with loathing. She scrambled to escape the mound, fleeing the cold rush of hatred with all her might. She dared not look back, yet she knew the horror edged ever closer. She could feel the evil at her heels, ready to consume her.

Fear stalked her. This horror was gaining on her. She knew that was true. The thicket was too far away. This thing was going to get her; it would rend her from ear to tail. It was just behind her. It was alongside her. It was going to get her – *now.*

In a blind rush, Bridget launched herself for the brush. She heard teeth snap for her legs – but she felt only her plunge through dark, wet branches.

She'd made it!

Thrilling awareness blocked off the pain of the stabbing bramble. She'd escaped, true enough, but she also knew the hellhound wouldn't give up. Bridget took shelter at the foot of the bush, hiding as best she could within its arms while she tried to figure out how she could get away.

Something surged through the branches at her feet. Within the darkness, Bridget discerned a long black snout, a pair of hungry green eyes, and rows of long white teeth.

Despair overwhelmed her. Bridget felt his hot breath, sensed his unyielding malevolence, and surrendered. Exhausted and broken, the effort to go on seemed beyond her, but even worse, it no longer appeared worth it. In her own eyes, she was a failure. She didn't deserve to live.

The large orbs flared. The jaws spread wide to devour her... and crumpled.

To Bridget's amazement, with a howl of rage and pain the giant head withdrew back into the darkness.

The young cat stood motionless in the shadows, awaiting her doom, half-doubting she'd seen what she'd seen. Yet from the world beyond she heard a battle raging in the trees. The hellhound snapped in great fury, only to yelp in anguish and frustration. Then he'd attack anew, and again get beaten back.

The draining uncertainty irritated Bridget. A singular thought held her mind: Why doesn't he just kill me and get it over with? But as the sounds of battle continued, it dawned on her that someone was doing an excellent job at holding off the hellhound. This was her chance to escape! And yet she knew it would never work, for her body was too worn down to evade the brute without help. *But isn't that what you have?* came an arresting thought. Like a taste of icy water, Bridget realized with great shock that it was true. Someone had come to rescue her!

"Scarface!" she cried out.

Forgetting her exhaustion, she stumbled out from under the brush. The hound spied her and charged, filling the night with his hateful snarls. Bridget collapsed against the mossy earth, quaking in fear, but before the black shepherd could reach her, a silvery form collided with the hound's dank snout. Together they crashed to the earth. His jaws snapped hard, and then screamed. In an aimless rush the hound fled, his tongue bleeding from where he'd bitten himself.

The silver form ran to Bridget, glowing as he bounded through the faint light. Then he caressed her. His touch was cold and hard.

Bridget could hardly believe it. "Sebastian?"

Without pause the small, glassy figurine started into the woods, motioning for her to follow.

"That's the wrong way," Bridget told him.

Sebastian took another couple of steps and again pointed forward with his head.

"But that's the way we came in!" she protested.

Sebastian didn't mind. On he ran, leaving Bridget to choose what she would do. But she was too weary to think. Confused and full of doubts, she rambled after the porcelain critter. Halfway back she stopped, rethinking the whole thing. Renewed snarls decided it for her.

Crawling under the fence, Bridget found Sebastian sitting in the dust, waiting for her.

"Thank you," she whispered.

Sebastian turned and ran.

"Wait!" Bridget called. "You're going backward again!"

The shimmering figure didn't care. On he went, picking up speed with each step. Watching him go, Bridget gave up her discontent and came along, placing her fate at his feet. When he changed paths, she followed – right into Jessica's backyard.

Of course, she'd never seen it from that view before, but she could recognize the house from its familiar smells.

"Wait," she mumbled, trying to catch her breath. "This makes no sense. Why didn't Scarface come this way?"

"Because he wanted you to die."

It was a horrible answer, harshly spoken, in tones that sounded hollow and unnatural. And yet Bridget heard deep compassion behind those words, and great sadness.

"Follow me," commanded Sebastian.

No longer questioning what he did, Bridget kept close as the limber figurine led her between two loose boards covering the eves to the crawlspace below the beaten rental house. Through nests of cobwebs and the trails of many mice they walked, until Sabastian crossed a series of cracks in deadwood boards and piled bricks to an eroded hole in a squared metal tube. He forced that open and entered, drawing Bridget into a long, black, rectangular tunnel. Closing the opening behind them, he led her into the darkness.

Lost and forgotten fur and dust billowed up with each step, clogging the stale air. Bridget held her breath as long as possible. Her heart rose with the effort, pounding from ear to ear. Against it, all she could hear was Sebastian's hard paws as he led her through a meandering passage that seemed to have no end.

A dim gray light appeared before them. The shiny cat stopped beneath a square of slashed metal that glowed from the world beyond. With a firm push, Sebastian wedged the pierced metal slab ajar enough for Bridget to crawl through. She recognized the place with a rush of great joy, but Sebastian didn't wait to share it. Letting the metal fall, he bounded up to his bookshelf nest before that dislodged air vent cover could slap back down against the floor.

Bridget listened as Jessica snapped alert on their padded board. The familiar sound filled her with joy. She was back! Back home! She'd survived!

"Thanks to Sebastian!" – a thought so strong, she spoke it aloud. With two great leaps, and one toppled picture frame, she was at his side.

"John!" Jessica began. "John! Wake up!"

As much as she loved hearing that, Bridget put it aside. Sebastian had curled up against the deadwood as if he might sleep long and hard. But he knew she was there.

"It has been my calling, and my pleasure, to keep a watch out for the Lady Jessica," he told Bridget through unmoving lips. "To guide her and protect her, in my own way. But my time is at end. Now it is yours."

"Mine?"

Sebastian drew his tail about his legs. Closing his eyes, solid lines started to form around his body. Even as he spoke, Bridget saw his limbs come together into one shiny mass.

"It is a great responsibility, Bridget, to serve among the angels. So now your selfishness, your petty hopes and fears, they all must end. For God Himself has chosen you to do this. Do not fail."

Bridget sat at his feet, patient, waiting, but Sebastian said no more. That's how John found her. Before she'd even realized he was there, John drew her to his chest.

"Honey!" he cried out. "It's Bridget!"

He hugged her, then seemed to think twice of that and held her aloft, his face squinting as if he'd punish her.

"Look at you!" he exclaimed. "Covered in lint! How did you –"

Jessica swept her from his hands. She kissed Bridget, saying a stream of loving incantations so quick, the cat couldn't understand a word of it. With the sleeve of her robe Jessica brushed the hairballs and dust off her beloved kitten. She rushed her into the kitchen, where she poured her young one bowls full of milk and food. Bridget touched the blessed snowy nectar with her tongue and recoiled, amazed Jessica still didn't grasp such a simple concept as her preferred milk temperature. And the food was the wrong type, too! But in the radiance of Jessica's love, it didn't matter. Purring so loud that it shook the hairs on her neck, Bridget rubbed against her beloved's almost hairless legs and felt content.

She was home.

Sixteen

That euphoria lasted a day or so.

Jessica pampered Bridget as the returned Prodigal Son, while John grit his teeth and looked the other way when Bridget rearranged the couch pillows or tossed aside that undesirable food they tried to feed her. But as the days rolled on, all the elements that had bothered Bridget surfaced anew. Jessica's homework

took ever more of her time. John forgot that he'd ever missed "the blasted cat." And the cramped, artificial world of their house seemed even more barren than before.

Worst of all, a smothering despair settled around Bridget each time she stepped a paw into the front room. It had once been her favorite place, but now, when she curled up in the windowsill, she would look at Sebastian's grave and remember what it had been like to smell the earth, prance across the dew-rinsed grass, and dig her claws into tree bark. She couldn't approach the metal air vent without wondering how she might slip through its black tunnels and escape once more to the outer world. She couldn't look at the bookshelves without thinking of the revelations from that figurine.

That, above all else, made no sense. Protect Jessica? When did the studious giant give Bridget a care anymore!

Many a time Bridget made a grand point of greeting her Jessica as the almost hairless one returned from her classes. The young cat would rub against Jessica's ankles or leap for her embrace, only to have the lady give her a few half-hearted pats and a gentle but determined shove aside. "Not now, Bridgey," Jessica would say. "I've got homework to do." Or "supper" or "laundry" or "dusting" or half a dozen other things.

At first, Bridget tried to be understanding. If she couldn't gain Jessica's affections, she could at least sit with her. But her lady soon decided she didn't like having a cat on her lap as she worked. Jessica needed the space for what she called her textbooks, folders, and portable computer, which to Bridget appeared like nothing more than a tiny, clackity picture window. So Bridget resigned herself to rest beside her beloved giant, but that seemed to mean nothing to Jessica. Bridget would take the time to settle into her nest – you know; adjusting her legs and spine just so, cleaning her hairs, making her neck and head comfy, which is all very important to a cat and can't be rushed – only to see Jessica gather her stuff, get up, and walk away. Just leaving Bridget there alone, for no reason at all.

It wasn't long before Bridget started doing things just to get Jessica's attention. Coughing up fur balls proved a natural place to begin, since Bridget had to put them somewhere. At first this worked well; the lady giant learned to come running with paper towels and cleaning fluid when she heard Bridget gagging. But as her studies increased, Jessica stopped worrying about arriving fur balls, figuring she'd just clean them up later. So even though Bridget herself didn't like their smell, she decided to stop limiting the foul lumps to select areas and started depositing them wherever she figured Jessica wouldn't want them. Like the pillows on their sleeping board, the kitchen counters, and the dining table.

That started out achieving her objective. Jessica did indeed respond at once to Bridget's coughs. But it came with a sharp, hostile attitude, one the cat didn't like. She decided to end this tactic when a soggy mess left atop the giant's homework almost brought Jessica to tears (however, Bridget did keep the practice up with John's papers).

That led the spotted feline to race through the house. You see, the deadwood floors ran from room to room in a small circle about the pantry. Bridget soon found that if she threw herself around that weird oval, charging full speed across the slick panels, her giants would sit still and watch her. Jessica would even call out encouragements to her cat. "Keep going – you'll get them!" she'd say. John

also paid attention to "her rampaging," as he'd refer to it, though he'd never respond unless Bridget lost control and collided with the wall panels or the furniture, to which he'd laugh with gusto.

Bridget soon found she couldn't do this very often. Her frequent impacts hurt, but beyond that, just running the circle had a strange effect on her stomach and head. Many times she'd discover she had to plop down and rest, to make sense of the spinning world. A nice twist to it all was that sometimes Jessica would bend down and lay the dizzy cat in her lap, petting her, but that never lasted long.

So Bridget took the next step and started knocking things over. The cat had tried to avoid this in the past, once she learned neither John nor Jessica liked picking things up, much less putting them away. But once she gave in to the urge, Bridget was surprised to find that batting down books, picture frames, and sugar bowls had many pleasing benefits. It got her giants' attention at all hours of the day or night, assuming one of them was there to hear the crash and see what was going on – and if not, it got their attention when they returned home. Even better, it proved quite fun!

Every room offered an abundant supply of targets. Some mornings John would pull on his artificial skins, only to wonder how his pocket doo-dads had ended up on the floor or behind the deadwood drawers. Bridget could have answered him if she'd understood all he'd said. Other days Jessica was left to mop up the shampoo that had fallen off the side of the tub, or refill the flowerpots that somehow slid out of the windowsills.

Bridget was especially amazed at how much she enjoyed watching boxes plunge off the refrigerator top. They would land with a muffled pop and an odd shuffling of their innards, which was a joy to hear, but once in a while, the packages themselves would explode against the deadwood floors, scattering white powder or little pieces of puffed sweets all over everything! That was just fascinating, seeing clouds build inside the kitchen and wondering if it would rain, or trying to figure out what kind of designs the scattering made. And then would inevitably follow the reunion with her giants, who would come into the kitchen on some aimless mission, only to find the floor cluttered with things that hadn't been there before. Bridget would sit atop the refrigerator, watching the mystery sparkle in their eyes, and then jump down to rub against their legs before they got mad. Still, that only worked a couple of times before her giants started getting angry anyway, so Bridget took to hiding after she knocked things off. It didn't earn her their affections, but it got their attention. And that, to the lonely cat, was worthwhile.

All this took a dynamic turn one night when John lay entrenched in his cushy lounger, the picture window blazing before him. Bridget came rampaging from the hall, determined to break the John paper toss factor (you see, he had taken to trying to hit her with a rolled-up newspaper as she'd race by), when all at once she spied the steaming mug he'd left on the deadwood counter beside his chair. It dawned on her that combining her attention-commanders might prove interesting, so Bridget pushed herself full-tilt towards the giant, then sprang for the mug. Upon impact the shiny cup flew right into John's lap, splattering brown liquid all over his chest.

Watching him howl in pain made Bridget want to jump for joy. It had worked far better than she'd ever dreamed possible! But when the feline tried to leap away, she couldn't slow down atop the polished table. Losing control, Bridget slid full speed into John's wet chest.

"YOU BLASTED CAT!" he screamed.

Jessica emerged from the kitchen. "What's going on here?" she exclaimed, although from the light twist in her voice, Bridget suspected she already had a good idea.

Bridget bounded off John's spongy artificial skin before he could grab her. But the bumbling giant surprised the agile cat, scrambling out of the lounger with unexpected fury. So Bridget scurried past her beloved into the kitchen. John pounded the floor in pursuit, shouting and waving a rolled-up pile of paper. Bridget threw herself up to the kitchen counter, then to the refrigerator top. Before she'd landed, John drew close enough to whack her tail with the newspaper. Bridget spat at him – he'd hit her hard! – and slid smack into a thick box.

"Not the Bisquick!" Jessica cried out as the container sprang off the edge.

Gritty powder billowed up from the kitchen floor. Bridget closed her eyes as the clouds passed by, leaving a thick trail of white dust.

The now-albino John brought his paper club down hard. Bridget dodged, not knowing what else to do. She had never seen him so angry! Gripped by fear, Bridget looked to Jessica, who was reaching for the broom in the corner. The cat had expected that; the lady always used that tool when the deadwood needed cleaning. But this time Jessica held the brush end upward. She pointed it at the refrigerator.

"That was a brand-new box!" she growled.

Bridget felt her heart chill. Her beloved giant was as angry as her volatile mate!

The cat shot into the bathroom as John swatted for her. Bridget couldn't believe what she saw. They hated her! How could this happen? They hated her! What could she do? They hated her!

She jumped atop the bedroom board. John swung for her bottom. Bridget switched directions and charged off, into the living room. John twisted to follow, lost his balance, and bowled into the bed.

Jessica passed him by, shouting Bridget's name over and over – but not from love.

In a blind rush, the cat leaped for the bookshelves. John had never been able to find her up there; perhaps Jessica couldn't, either. Plowing through two picture frames atop the cabinet top, Bridget threw herself to the second shelf, then bounded again to the top. There she curled into the corner, trembling, expecting the club or broom to pummel her at any moment. Instead, she heard something shatter. Jessica gasped, then started crying.

The sound of her beloved's sudden hurt erased Bridget's every concern. She rushed to the side, peering down to see what had wounded Jessica so.

Half-bathed in white powder, her favorite giant knelt against the deadwood, weeping. In her hands, Jessica cradled pieces of the porcelain Sebastian.

John laid a comforting hand on her shoulder. "We'll get another one," he whispered.

"It won't be the same," Jessica moaned.

Breathing deep, John looked around the room, as if he were searching for something. He glanced up. His eyes focused on Bridget. She cringed.

It wasn't a harsh look his white face cast, or even an angry one, and yet the determination within his gaze filled her with dread.

She sprang off the bookshelf, intent only on escaping. She landed on the air vent. One extended claw caught under its edge and popped the metal up.

Bridget dove inside.

Seventeen

"So… you finally figured it out."

Bridget didn't bother to turn towards the interloper. As much as she loathed that voice, she had more important things to consider.

She sat shivering in the darkness beneath the house, her fur coated with white powder, old dust balls, and what John had called lint. Her breath turned to fog before her eyes.

Bridget never imagined it could get so cold. It was never like this in the house.

Scarface laughed. "Oh, it gets much worse. Wait till you see snow!"

Bridget had no idea what he was talking about, but from the way he said it, she knew she wouldn't like it.

Scarface took a seat beside her. Bridget felt his warmth and drew near, then realized what she was doing and pulled away.

His tail whipped about with his frustration and disappointment. "What's wrong?"

"I want nothing to do with you!" she snapped.

"Oh? Well, it looks to me like you're going to be needing me, sugar."

"I don't need you!"

"Oh, yeah? Then why don't you go back in, if you're so cold?" His eyes arched in triumph. "I'll tell you why. Because you don't know how – do you?"

Bridget wanted to slap his face, adding her own claw marks to his nose and cheek, but she couldn't. He was right. She'd been lucky just to find Sebastian's hole after stumbling and choking through those horrid black tunnels. She wouldn't dare think of doing it again.

A chill breeze swept by, accenting her foreboding. Why oh why had she done all those things in there? How did she end up in this mess?

"And I'll tell you something else," Scarface said. "You wouldn't want to be back there anyway. She'll never forgive you, breaking her statue like that."

"But I didn't mean to!"

"You think that matters? Wake up, kid! You're no different than the rest of us!

Once you start growing up, all that love they showed you just blows away. You're not the cute little squirt you were when they picked you out and brought you home. Now you're some large, hungry, troublesome beast. And a klutz to boot."

Bridget drew her tail tight around her. She didn't want to think about this. Not at all. Jessica wasn't like that!

"Go away," she whispered.

The scruffy cat chuckled. "You sheltered ninny! I'm trying to help you!"

"Help me? You tried to kill me!"

Scarface stiffened, though his tail twitched a bit in nervous tension he soon contained.

"Why would you think that?" he asked, his words dark.

"Sebastian told me."

"Sebastian? He's been dead for months!" The calico feline drew himself up to his full height. With a defiant flip of an ear he turned, walking away, but by his fourth step he'd hesitated, and by his sixth he'd looked back to face her. "If I'd wanted you dead, I wouldn't have helped you escape the dragon. I wouldn't have guided you out of the street. As God is my witness, I could kill you now, little one! But I won't.

"You arrogant little squirt – alive a whole five months and already you think you know everything there is to know! Fool! You accuse me? You know nothing. NOTHING! You've never even been out like this before – in the real world. You have no idea what it takes to survive out here, with no one to feed you, to curl up to and sleep with. No idea. But you'll learn. Oh yes. You'll soon be living with ticks between your ears and fleas trampling through your matted fur, straggling around for days in mud and sweat. Just trying to find some little corner where you can get out of the wind and rain, where you can have just a minute's peace. Digging through discarded trash for old, rotting scraps these people throw away."

With each word Scarface said, Bridget cringed ever closer to the hard earth. Did he speak the truth? Was that what it was like to live out here? To have this "freedom" she'd longed for?

Each point he raised terrified her, until she could take it no more.

"Oh no I won't!" she cried. "I'll – I'll – I'll catch mice, and birds!"

Scarface leaned back and laughed. "You? You can't even toss your master's cup without landing in the mess you make! Do you have any idea how hard it is to catch a grasshopper, much less a mouse? No, my silly friend, you'll hit the

garbage like all the rest of us. Take my word for it – a trash bag doesn't run away, hide in holes, or just disappear. It doesn't even defend itself. Yes, that's what you'll take – what's left of it, anyway."

"What's left? What do you mean?"

"Why, you don't think all the other cats are just going to give you their supper, do you? Oh no, my little Bridget, you'll have to fight for it – and for your bed, your water. Everywhere you'll go, there's going to be someone who'll kill just to take your space or your food. If you're not a good warrior, you'll die quick."

Hot tears started rolling down her cheeks, only to turn ice cold in the night air. Bridget tried to rub her eyes dry, not wanting Scarface to see her crying. Everyone knew warriors didn't cry. And yet that meant little to her now. Desperate to understand everything he'd said, one devastating question haunted her: What kind of hell had she forced her way into?

Through the chill breeze, Bridget heard stiff, muffled footfalls. Between cracks in the crumbling sideboards, she saw John's slippers, his robe.

"You sure she's out here?" came Jessica's voice.

"She must be," John answered. "There must be a hole in the furnace tubes somewhere under the house." His feet shuffled about as he turned around. "That would also explain our heating bills," he mumbled.

Scarface rose to his feet. "Come on. I'll get you out of here."

"Oh no," Bridget rebelled. "I'm not following you again!"

The elder cat stared deep into her eyes. "If you stay here, John will punish you. And he'll screw that vent back down, so you won't be able to get out again. You'll be stuck in there, a prisoner, and you'll never get free because they won't trust you. They learn quickly, these humans, when they want to – and they've seen how you got past them. It won't work again."

Bridget shivered against the cold earth. She didn't want to think about any of this. It was all wrong! She'd wished it had never happened.

Perhaps if she just sat there, and closed her eyes, this would all disappear. She'd awake from another bad dream.

"They'll always be watching you," said Scarface, shattering her blind hopes. "They never forget what hurts them, and they never forgive. Why should they? You're not the squirt they loved."

"He never loved me!" Bridget interrupted.

"You're just a big, awkward mess that breaks their toys and eats their food and smells up their house and grows fleas and attacks them when they're not expecting it. They'll tolerate you – nothing more."

John bellowed out Bridget's name. Strange, it lacked any trace of anger or hatred.

"Hear how sweet he sounds?" Scarface whispered. "He's trying to lure you out."

The giant shuffled his feet ever closer, even as Jessica's sorrowful voice called for her pet. Bridget trembled in self-pity and fear. *Oh God*, she prayed, *I don't know what to do!*

A twig snapped. Bridget jumped to her feet as only a cat can, hoping beyond hope she'd find Sebastian had once more come to save her. But Bridget knew in her heart that was impossible. He'd said so – and besides, she'd destroyed his vessel.

With all that was going on, she began to wonder if she'd ever really met Sebastian. Maybe it was all just her imagination.

"Now follow me!" Scarface commanded. "This is our last chance!"

She just stood there, frozen in agony, so the big calico cat swatted her rear end with his left front claws. That made her leap forward, but before she'd landed, he was at her side, encouraging her. Together they scampered across the backyard, passing the shepherd fence to the forbidding black road and the field beyond. Scarface guided her through the glow of a corner streetlight until they'd reached a cove of thick brush under a spreading elm. Bridget was glad to rest there, for her muscles ached and her mind still fought to stay afloat within her despair. Scarface huddled among the branches, happy to be out of the breeze, and yet he knew one task remained before him.

The hardest one of all.

"A tough old bat named Carl lives here," he said, stretching his legs, "so if I were you, I'd continue down this road."

Bridget snapped upright. She'd have laughed if she'd seen herself, for she'd looked just like Jessica startled from her sleep on a cold night. But this wasn't a laughing matter.

"You're leaving me?" she blurted out.

He nodded with some honest regret. "Have to, kid. My territory ended way back there. If Carl smells me, he'll come to fight. He'll tackle you, too, if he finds you, so you'd better hurry. Don't worry – the humans have a big playground just

around the corner, with an old porch you can sleep under and a brook you can drink from. You can practice hunting birds and squirrels there, with all the big trees hanging around, and when you fail, there's usually some trash nearby. Just watch out for Butch."

"Butch?" she squealed, hating everything he'd suggested. "What's a butch?"

"And Tiger. And the hawk."

"No, wait! I don't want to do this!"

The fur tensed along his spine. Scarface rose hard and stiff above her.

"What did you think was going to happen – we were just going to find a house of our own? You can't stay with me, kid. There isn't enough food, and there are always other cats trying to cut a piece of my territory. I can't have you slowing me down. So go on! This is your chance! Be a warrior! Run!"

Bridget felt tears rushing down her face. She didn't care.

Why oh why did this have to happen to her?

"Go on, you fool!" Scarface spat. "You want Carl to kill you? He will, if he smells you. So go – NOW!"

He reared swift as a serpent, spreading wide his fur and fangs like the great killer beast she'd always imagined he was. In pure terror Bridget fled from him, bolting into the unknown. Scarface – which, by the way, was not what he called himself – watched her disappear in solemn silence. Only as mist rose from the roadway, chilling him to the bone, did the old cat rise to return home. He moaned at his distasteful deed. She had been a good squirt... kind of cute, to be honest. In a couple of seasons, he might have welcomed her. But not now. As much as it had hurt him, Scarface knew in his heart that it had to end this way. After all, *he* was Sebastian's rightful heir.

Eighteen

Bridget ran until her pads cracked and her toes bled, and then she ran some more.

Terror drove her – a primal, overwhelming dread of every light and shadow, every bush, cricket's chirp, and whistling breeze. She had no idea where she was going. She couldn't even remember where that treacherous Scarface had suggested she head. Nor did she care. She clung to the jet-black dragon path, following it where it would lead. She had to, for as soon as she had fled, a murky fog separated her from the rest of God's world like a wall of dire forbidding. So she ran along the path's banks, rounding one curve, then another, up one hill and down another. Chill droplets formed in her fur, and her throat burned from the icy mist, but Bridget rambled on, hounded by her fears. It didn't take long for the greatest of these to catch up with her. She felt its approach in the soft ashen rock, a deep quivering of power and mass. Then the gaze of its starry eyes fell across her

back, and she knew a dragon had found her. Bridget threw her weary frame forward, not daring to look back, and yet she could feel the beast closing on her, its stomach churning with lust for her flesh. Within moments it would catch her.

So the one decision Bridget dreaded, she made without a second thought. She swerved off the depressed path as she heard the dragon's feet grinding the road at her back. As two suns its eyes burned through the dazzling fog, but in an onrushing thunder they passed by and disappeared. Bridget was left lost and alone in the black mist.

That's how she faced the choice of what to do, where to go. In truth, Bridget didn't want to choose at all; she had a powerful yearning to curl up in the fog and wait to see what she could at daybreak – if she survived that long. But against her fears remained some strand of her stubborn independence, and that bulwark figured she knew her way back to the dragon's dead zone. After some hesitation and debate, Bridget gave in and moved. Two sets of ten steps later, it became apparent she wasn't where she'd expected to be. She stopped, retraced her route, and went a different way. The result was the same – the stark terror of being all alone in an alien land.

"Why?" she cried out, knowing only God could hear her. "Why did this have to happen to me?"

Words from the past echoed through her mind. *So now your selfishness, your petty hopes and fears, they all must end. For God Himself has chosen you to do this. Do not fail.*

Bridget wept. She had her answer.

It was so clear now. Sebastian had charged her with that command, to "guide and protect the Lady Jessica." And yet Bridget had fallen victim to her selfish nature almost as soon as he'd gotten her back home – demanding Jessica's attention when her beloved giant couldn't give it, disregarding the wondrous protections her giants provided, coveting what she didn't need and couldn't have. On all counts, she had failed.

Her memories chanted on. *It has been my calling, and my pleasure, to keep a watch out for the Lady Jessica.... But my time is at an end....*

"Okay!" Bridget screamed. "I'm sorry already!"

It is a great responsibility, Bridget, to serve among the angels.... Now it is yours....

"Oh, Lord," she whispered, "I'm so sorry."

Now it is yours....

"Agh! What more do you want from me?"

Now it is yours....

"I said I was sorry. I am! But I don't know what I can do about it now! I don't even know where I am!"

Now it is yours....

Bridget could almost feel Sebastian beside her, speaking words as crushing as boulders. She recalled how he'd come to her in the shepherd's woods, beckoning her to follow.

Now it is yours....

All at once she could see him, a shimmering ghost in the cold, damp air. Silent, unimposing, Sabastian came as he had before – motioning for her to follow, then disappearing into the mist.

Bridget felt her heart quiver, her muscles shake. A great weariness swept through her bones. Sleep summoned her.

"I'm dreaming," she whispered. "That must be it."

Even as she said this, Bridget knew it was no dream, but self-condemnation. She was dredging up the painful past because she had failed God, Sebastian, and Jessica. Bridget deserved all she had brought upon herself. She deserved to die.

The phantasm drew near once more, motioning for her to follow. Bridget shuttered her eyes. The vision was too painful to behold.

"Lord, forgive me," she said, collapsing to the wet grass. "I have sinned against you. I am undone."

"No, my child," came His gentle reply. "You are redeemed. Now come with Me."

Nineteen

The ghostly form bounded into the fog. Bridget staggered after him. Passing by a hill of grass, the little silver figure sprang through sharp weeds as tall as John's knees. Tiny needles pierced Bridget's flanks as she followed. Then Sebastian dove into a wall of dense shrubbery. Limping from the weed spurs and her broken pads, Bridget paused at the brush line. The stiff leaves were so thick, she couldn't see ahead.

Sebastian was gone.

"Lord, protect me," she whispered. Then she jumped in, and plummeted.

You see, the thicket had been a natural wall atop a steep hillside. Bridget rolled through stubborn branches that cut like sharp blades into her thighs and calves. Now understand, the brush had endured regular trims, so it was kept no wider than one of Bridget's mightier jumps. Even so, it seemed like a stabbing eternity before the young cat came to a rough and tumble halt in a bed of freshly mowed grass, sweet with dew. From somewhere nearby she heard a rush of water.

Bridget tried to stand. Her head rocked about as if it was still twisting over and over down the slope.

"Youh awlwight?" came a shrill voice.

The ailing cat tried to leap to an alert stance, but in her weary and broken state, only her back legs responded. Bridget ended up flipping through an awkward roll onto her back, plopping into the soggy grass.

"Youh awlwight?" repeated the call.

"Obvioudly she awlwight," answered another.

"She not sayh so," replied the first.

"Youh teacht me that?" said still another. "Oh yes, yesss, I think she teacht me that. It looked fun, it did. Yes, oh yess!"

To Bridget's surprise, the pain of her fall helped settle her dizzy brain, and that allowed her to identify the voices. She'd heard such speech before from the mice in Jessica's pantry. That's how she halfway understood what this group was saying. And yet there was something different about it.

She glanced about. The fog was thin at the base of the hill, giving her a bigger field of vision, and yet she couldn't find the tiny black eyes or stringy flopping tails that usually gave away hidden mice. But there was a shuffling in the grass, a visible movement in the stalks and clippings – and it was heading towards her.

That struck her odd. Mice wouldn't dare approach her. They wouldn't move at all, unless she was chasing them.

The whole thing grew through her lingering fears into a troubling dilemma.

"Hold there!" she cried out. "Come no closer!"

Four heads popped up, staring at her with curious eyes. Then four more heads appeared. Then five. They looked like mice, but they were huge – about half

Bridget's size – with big, fidgeting teeth and peculiar wiggling noses.

"Rats!" Bridget screamed, leaping away.

"Heyh, where's she going?" a newcomer called.

Huge trunks of elm, oak, and walnut loomed around her, upholding a canopy of countless green, brown, and red leaves. Bridget left the grassy field behind for their misty shadows. Glancing back, she saw a multitude of shapes the size of John's hands, all of them scurrying after her.

"Sebastian!" the frightened feline yelled. "Sebastian, where are you?"

The earth rose before her. Through a pile of dead leaves and twigs she ran, when all of a sudden the ground gave way, and she fell into a pool of marsh sand. Beyond it swirled a gurgling channel of cold water, its girth and depth surpassing the tub Jessica used for Bridget's irregular immersions.

A black shadow charged over Bridget's head. She glanced up but did not see the swooping form. By the whistle of its wings, she recognized it as a bird, though it had been like no flier she'd ever witnessed. From its dark outline, Bridget suspected it must have been twice her size.

"Lord have mercy," she whispered.

A harsh, piercing call tore through her. It came from the winds, like the robin's song, but had no grace or harmony. Even so, Bridget knew it for what it was – the scream of a hunter.

She huddled against the bank, staring into the misty treetops. Somewhere up there, she knew, was a great bird of prey.

Again she felt the wellspring of panic and dismay bubble forth inside her, but this time Bridget fought it down. She understood the ways of the hunter, so the young cat knew that if she gave in to her fears, if she turned her back and fled, the attacker would have her. But if Bridget moved with caution and care, keeping her eyes alert, she had a chance.

A squirrel started chattering above her. Bridget located the critter hanging from an elm branch, clutching an acorn in her front paws as her thick, bushy tail curled about the limb above. The little squirrel took a bite of the shell, then tossed the piece onto Bridget's head. It landed with a soft smack and slid down her back to rest on her tail, even as another slab of shell impacted her ear.

Though irritated, Bridget said nothing. She didn't know squirrel speech, and she had no wish to call more attention to herself. But when the squirrel threw a bit of acorn shell hard into her left eye, Bridget gave in to her anger and charged up

the slope. At least she tried to, only to feel something latch hard onto a patch of her tail hair. To Bridget's fortune, the trap didn't hold; her surge had been strong enough to yank free the snagged fur. Still, it hurt like anything.

Bridget twisted about, set to teach this unwanted interloper a lesson. Her anger wilted before what she saw. For down on the sand was the strangest thing the cat ever imagined. It looked like a circular bone extending out of the water. Its wet gray-green form sat where Bridget had been, its frame curled like her old food dish turned inside out. But its stiff, shiny surface rose and fell in great, rippling spikes. Along its crest lay three great holes. From the center one extended a piece of bone with two hard, fearless eyes and a beak the size of Bridget's head. In its mouth lay the cat's lost fur.

Chirping in anger, the squirrel tossed an acorn bit at the water monster. The chip struck the shelled serpent's snout and bounced away. To Bridget's amazement, the creature did not respond. The bony head slid inside its bowl-like body and disappeared.

"Old Snappy! Old Snappy!" cried a rat, one of many that had appeared around Bridget on the crest.

The squirrel gave a long squeal.

"She warned youh," a rat told Bridget. "Gott to listen. Yes, yessss! Ghot to listen."

"Watch Old Snappy," said another.

Not knowing what to say or do, Bridget charged into the woodlands. What was this place God had led her to, with big giant birds and herds of rats and attacking squirrels and bony water monsters? Was this hell? Her own private little hell?

A giant shadow loomed before her. In sudden fear Bridget slid to a halt. This new thing dwarfed her, the hill, even the trees! It was horrendous, rearing like a mountain, with four lofty arms stretching out in all directions! But then the winds changed, and she caught its scent. It was deadwood! Real deadwood! Bridget sprang forward with glee. Sliced and assembled deadwood meant but one thing – shelter! For this place had been made by hairless giants!

As she drew near, Bridget could smell the giants' presence, but it seemed faint and old. This deadwood also differed from what she'd known before, lacking the oil coats, colors, and dusty eddies that marked Jessica's home. The grayed boards and planks supporting this massive structure seemed bare to the wind and rain, and thus suffered from far more decay. But that didn't matter, Bridget decided. It

still promised shelter.

Bridget circled the circular edifice, checking it out. On three sides it bordered the trees and grass, but along the edge with the sealed wall hole, she found a dragon's dead zone. That space was empty now, though Bridget could still smell the burned oil and acid drool in the soft rock. Dragons must have slept there, at one time or another.

Unlike Jessica's home, Bridget found no places where she could escape beneath the structure. It appeared solid all the way around, despite its age and decay. But on one side the deadwood sides had been pulled back, though the top remained. It reminded Bridget of what Jessica's front room would have been like if the transparent wall had not even existed. She stepped beneath the cover to find no path down to the deadwood floor. The earth simply plunged, so she jumped down. At once she noticed the air warmed, its movement slowed to a crawl. This change thrilled her. These deadwood sides protected her from the cooling breeze!

Falling in love with the place, Bridget thanked God for bringing her there. She curled up in a dark, secluded corner under a sturdy bench. Though dusty, with a few cobwebs, the shelter warmed her, and its isolation helped her block out the horrors beyond. She felt at peace.

As her eyes drew to a close, she spied movement in the far shadows.

Bridget stiffened, focusing on the darkness. The black specter approached with slow, cautious steps, its body hanging close to the drop-wall.

Uncertainty gripped Bridget. She couldn't make out what the thing was, since it stayed clear of the light, and she couldn't hope to escape, as it crept ever between Bridget and the outer world. So the cat laid there, trying not to tremble, hoping whatever it was wouldn't see her. And yet she knew that was impossible – each stride proved it knew her location!

On came the intruder, step by step. Bridget fought to contain her boiling frustrations. Why doesn't it charge? Come on, she almost called – end this! Rush me! Give me an opening! Oh, come on! Make a move! At least give me a chance to flee!

At that moment the fog must have broken, if only for a second, but it was enough for a moonbeam to fall upon that cavity in the deadwood. It illuminated two huge, flopping ears of rich, brassy fur, hanging from a shaggy head bigger than Bridget's entire body.

With the light upon him, the rust-red hound realized he was exposed and rose up, issuing a low growl that pulsated from wall to wall.

Bridget knew that she was about to die.

$\mathscr{T}$*wenty*

The wolfhound charged, snarling and barking up a crescendo that could crush eardrums without even trying to. Bridget sprang up in a dreadful fright, hit her head against the deadwood bench, and collapsed.

The long-haired hound stopped hard.

"Scared her," said a rat, lifting his head at the ledge above. "Yes, yesss. Scared her good."

"Awlready scared she was," put in another.

"Scared her good," repeated the first.

"I did, didn't I?" agreed the dog. His chest surged in pride. "That was one of my better ones, I think."

"Oh, the poor dear," said the squirrel, scampering down to Bridget's side. As you might expect, the squirrel was quite cautious, for this wise little critter had lived in the park longer than all the others, and so she knew the humbled young cat would strike out with terror if she were in any way alert. But that, at least, the squirrel didn't have to worry about. Bridget was sound asleep with a big bump atop her skull. So as the elder of the woods, the squirrel did what she had to do. Turning toward the giant golden retriever, she snapped, "Butch, how many times must I tell you not to treat strangers that way?"

The big hound melted under her scrutiny.

"Ah, but Edna, I've got to practice on somebody," he pleaded. "You know I'd never have hurt her."

"Yes, I know that," the squirrel allowed.

"We awl know that," squeaked a rat.

"Yes, yesss, we do," agreed another. And the rest all chimed in.

"But you can't just go around scaring things like that," Edna the squirrel continued. "Look at her! She's all cut up and hurting."

"Old Snapper tried to ghet her!" said another rat.

"He did! He did! He did!" sang the rats.

Butch hung his head to the ground. "But Edna, no one's scared of me."

"Yes," Edna sighed. "Yes, well. I know, Butch dear, I know. Don't let it bother you. You're a good, loving dog. That's what's important; remember that."

"I know," Butch moaned, "but once, just once...."

Edna wasn't listening. "Now, this spotted one.... It looks to me like she was hurting long before Snapper. Yes, well. That doesn't matter now, does it? She's here now, and she needs our help."

"Humph!" crowed the hawk, who landed on the upper ledge and let himself hang upside-down so he could better view the festivities. "Looks to me like she needs the Stumper."

"The Stumper!" screamed the rats. "The Stumper!"

"Hates us, he does!" said one.

"Yes," said Edna, considering. "Well, I don't know if I'd say hate, but even so, you'll just have to forgive him that. But I think you're right; we'll need him. But we've also got to do what we can now."

Edna crawled up to Bridget, feeling her ear and listening to her breathing. Then she drew back to the hound, who still knelt in sadness at her feet.

"Butch, you lick her wounds up all you can, and keep her warm. Show her your food and water bowl if she feels up to it. Agnes," she said to the largest rat, "you all keep an eye out for the Stumper."

"Humph!" called the hawk. "I'll see him before they do!"

"You're often gone in the mornings," Edna replied.

"Humph!" snapped the hawk. "Don't trust me, huh?"

"And why should I? I saw you dive over this little one."

"Humph! Maybe someday I'll dive over you!"

The rats scolded him for that, though Edna only laughed. It was the hawk, after all, who kept the park free of all the ruffian dogs, cats, skunks, snakes, and other rogues who might prey on its citizens. Butch, on the other paw, couldn't even harm a tick on his head. God bless him, the hound was too gentle in his soul for such tasks.

"But Edna," Butch cut in, "can't I be scary some time? Please?"

By Kirby Lee Davis

Twenty-one

Have you ever awakened feeling everything in this world was just about perfect?

That may be a rare event for many of you, since humans have such a limited conception of our Creator's perfection and therefore rarely praise God for just how cool a place this is. But the animals never had a falling out with our Lord, and so they find contentment in the simplest of things.

That's how Bridget returned to us.

She'd been dreaming about long-forgotten groomings from her mother and father, though she no longer recognized them as her parents, having no actual recollection of them in that way. But somewhere deep in that feline mind, she retained cherished impressions of the love and security she'd felt each time they'd licked her and cuddled her and combed her until she was just about perfect. It was that memory she was reliving when awareness returned after that dreadful night. And it was that memory that kept her from panicking herself to a stroke when she realized it was Butch licking, cuddling, and combing her.

She jerked up at that thought, opening her eyes to find the golden retriever's enormous head rocking her this way and that, his thick black and maroon tongue rolling a syrupy stream of drool across her hurts, his bulbous nose puffing hot, dank breath through her spotted fur. The shock of it all made Bridget forget how good his efforts felt. All she wanted was to run as far away as possible, but just thinking about lifting her legs hurt, and each time she took the painful jolt and tried, the huge snout nudged her back into place, its touch soft yet firm.

Something chirped beside her. The hound's reddish snout rolled Bridget over, so that her head lay snug atop one of his soft, giant paws. From that view, the cat could see the squirrel sitting beside the hound's flank on the deadwood floor, watching them in the morning twilight. That squirrel chirped again, and the dog snorted a hot blast that Bridget welcomed against her soggy chest. Then the squirrel scampered away.

"She's awake!" called a rat. "She's awake!"

The big hound lifted her snout, coughed, and went back to licking Bridget's sore, torn thighs. To her surprise, the feline found she kind of liked all this. It helped, of course, if she closed her eyes.

"I'm not bawthering her," the rat snapped at the hound.

"Might be," another rat said.

"Am not," the first cut back.

"Might be."

"Am not!"

The hound leaned his head back and let loose a thunderous bark. Bridget tried to shut her ears, but the harsh sound still hurt.

The squirrel bounded over the ledge, running to a perch right atop the dog's giant skull. The fox-tailed rodent chattered. The dog nodded with such power, the squirrel rolled down to the hound's rusty tail.

"Oh, wow," called a rat. "Youh teacht me that?"

"Youh teacht me that too?" a chorus of others joined in.

The squirrel scolded them. Without a word, the rats started backing from the forest ledge. It took Bridget a moment to realize they were leaving.

"No, wait!" she called.

One of the rats hesitated, looking her way with curious eyes, but Bridget had no chance to call to him. Butch chose that moment to wash her face, which blinded the young cat.

"Want something youh want?" the rat called.

Bridget coughed, then snorted the drool out of her nose. Butch didn't mind, turning his attention to her ears.

"Yes," Bridget said when she could get a sound out. "You can speak with these... these... with them?"

"Oh, yes, yesss, yessss!" the rat called, overjoyed to be talking with her.

"How?" Bridget wanted to know.

"How what?"

"How do you do it?"

The rat seemed perturbed. "I learn. Yes, oh yesss. I learn much!"

Settling down on the deadwood beside the hound, the squirrel issued a long list of chirps to the rat.

"I am being nice!" the rat protested.

Again Butch cleansed her face with his stinky, slug-like tongue. With his paw

holding her down, and her body aching pretty much every way possible, Bridget didn't know what else she could do but put up with it. And besides, it felt good.

"But how – " Bridget paused to clear her nose once more – "how do you talk with them?"

The rat stood upright on the ledge. "Now youh listen," he snapped. "Howa long youh lived here, huh?"

Bridget thought that a stupid question. "Not even a day!"

"Yeah!" the rat stated. "Well, awlwight then."

"All right what?"

"I live here a lot longer than youh. Lot longer, yes, yess, yesss!"

The squirrel chattered something that spurred the rat to sit down once more. Then the squirrel crawled up to Bridget, looking over her cuts and scrapes. She cheeped again and again.

"She wants to know how youh get so hurt," the rat said.

Bridget really didn't know. "Just traveling, I guess."

"From where? From where?"

Bridget didn't know that, either. "A long ways," she said.

The rat repeated that, to which the squirrel and hound traded chirps and soft barks.

"That was something youh did," the rat proclaimed. "Both them, they think that."

The hound pulled his head back to stare into Bridget's face with his deep brown orbs. The young cat felt a jolt of fear, but as the long-haired dog just sat there, observing her, Bridget realized a sense of peace. It wasn't the love she felt just being around Jessica, whom she now missed so much that it hurt her inside, but still, the dog's stare did comfort her.

"He thinks youh some sort of warrior, a great warrior, to make such a, a journey, to bear such wounds. Like the hawk," the rat explained. Then he hesitated. "But he wonders... he wonders something. He wonders something of youh... he wonders if he scared youh. When youh first see him."

"If he scared me?"

Her curiosity piqued, Bridget looked first at the rat, who seemed a little embarrassed, then at the hound, who sat before her, hanging on the answer. His intense stare made her smile.

"Yes," Bridget admitted. "Tell him he almost scared me to death."

The rat repeated that, not realizing just how true it was. The dog cast a curious stare at the rat, who nodded as if defending the accuracy of his translation. Then the big hound crawled even closer to Bridget, wrapped his forelegs around her and laid his head across her body, just as he might one of his own beloved puppies.

Although surprised and somewhat alarmed, Bridget soon fell into a deep and contented sleep. Caught up within his overwhelming warmth, she didn't hear the stampede of rats around the shelter, each one screeching, "The Stumper! The Stumper!"

Twenty-two

Deeply satisfied, Scarface crawled under the house to watch the setting sun. It had been a glorious day. Everything was falling into place, just as he'd planned.

Sebastian's Lady Jessica had spent her waking hours sobbing for a cat that wouldn't return. John tried to console her, but they'd both known that was just talk. The truth was, taking on Bridget had stretched their resources to the limit. They couldn't afford to replace her.

After a few days – maybe a week – Scarface expected Jessica to start putting good food out for him again, and not that stale stuff she'd been substituting in his back-porch bowl ever since Bridget came on the scene. Maybe Jessica would start giving him a little milk now and then, too, when John wasn't looking, just like she had before. And then, maybe after another week, the lady would resume those little play sessions they used to enjoy. She'd come out to sit on the porch, talking to him and petting him, tossing him sticks and leaves and artificial mice.

John might have suspected, but he'd never truly realized just how much care Jessica had poured out on Scarface. For the moment, the gnarled alley veteran thought that was best. But if all went according to plan, if Scarface played his part just right, the Fergusons would soon realize that adopting him as their own would be a good thing to do. After all, he could be just as loving as the next cat, when he needed to be.

You see, long, long ago, Scarface recognized just how precious a creature Jessica was, and how good a home she could provide. Sebastian had often enchanted him with glorious tales of the foods she would make or the massages she would give. That's one reason Scarface staked out the Ferguson household as his sovereign territory, for he knew Sebastian couldn't live forever.

It didn't concern Scarface when an old man came walking up the cracked and broken sidewalk, making more noise with his cane clattering on the concrete than did his soft, shuffling shoes. The newcomer stepped with purpose into the yard, pausing a bit at Sebastian's grave before rambling up to the front door. Curious, Scarface followed him. The dusty cat got around the corner just in time to see the man rap that portal with his cane.

John opened the door. Surprise flashed across his face.

"Well, hello, Mr. Scabbard! How are you?"

"I'm fine, Mr. Ferguson, though I'm wondering about you right now."

That got John's attention. "Why would you worry about us?"

"I'm not," the old man snapped, hanging his cane onto his forearm. "But I'm afraid you're missing something."

Scarface flexed his claws in anger. What was this interloper doing?

"So we are!" John exclaimed. Calling his wife to the door, he turned back and asked, "Do you know where she is?"

"Oh yes. I saw the little thing this morning down at the park, in the storage area under the old windmill."

A pink-faced Jessica came alongside her mate, slipping her arms around John's back. The old man nodded, extended a hand. She took it in hers, shaking them both.

"Mrs. Ferguson? I'm Jason Scabbard. I own the pet shop where John here got your kitten."

"He knows where she is!" John proclaimed.

New life flowed into Jessica's eyes. "Oh, thank God!" Then she hesitated, as if torn. "But... I don't understand. Why didn't you just bring her back?"

"Well, Mrs. Ferguson, I care about the animals I sell. When I found her this morning clawed and bruised – "

"She's hurt?" Jessica blurted out.

Jason smiled as he continued. " – I just had to make sure she wasn't being mistreated. I can see by your reactions that you care about her. That's all I wanted

to know."

Jessica batted back tears. "Oh, please come in, Mr. Scabbard! Please tell us all about it!"

They disappeared into the house, but Scarface didn't hang around to watch. He realized now he'd made a great mistake not killing Bridget when he had the chance. *Drat those shepherds for letting her get away! Drat Carl and Butch and the hawk! What's wrong with this world, anyway? You can't count on anyone anymore!*

But that didn't matter now, did it? No, it didn't, Scarface admitted to himself. But he hadn't lost yet.

Oh, he knew the risks before him. Just as soon as they came to their senses, Jessica would herd John down to the park, they'd rescue their precious Bridget, and Scarface would lose his last chance for a comfortable life. For love and food and happiness.

Harnessing his anger for the unpleasantness ahead, Scarface sprinted out of the yard. There was still hope, if he got to the park first. Then he could finish the task.

Twenty-three

Bridget found the pain had lessened enough by the end of the day that she could bear small walks. Her pads still ached, and she feared the cuts on her legs would start bleeding again if she did anything too stressful, but even so, it felt so good to stand up once more. Butch was so happy he licked out her ears a fourth time, which bothered Bridget almost as much as his big shaggy tail knocking her down with every swing. And yet, she found herself liking the loving hound.

The squirrel sat atop the deadwood bench, her sharp eyes watching as Bridget walked her sluggish legs across the depressed floor. Edna chirped one phrase, then another. Bridget stopped to await the rat's translation.

"She sayhs maybe with the new dayh, youh can leev here," he said. "If youh wish."

That made Bridget pause. She hadn't considered staying, but in truth, she

didn't know what she was going to do. Her heart so wanted to go back and confront Scarface, but she was afraid, and still too weak. She didn't feel able to make even the leap up to the forest ledge!

The squirrel chattered some more. "She sayhs youh most welcome to stay," the rat explained. "Most welcome. And we all agree. Yes, yesss. Most welcome youh are."

Bridget half-expected the chorus to join in on that. She felt disappointed when they didn't.

"Where is everyone?" she asked.

The squirrel chirped an answer. Bridget couldn't help smiling at how the little thing had learned to understand her in but a day. Bridget didn't think she'd ever learn squirrel speech.

"There's some, some... commotion, yess, that's it! Commotion in the streets around," the rat said. "Tom'alaxt, he circles above. My brothers and sisters, they keep watch. So do her folk."

Butch flung himself over the ledge. The squirrel cheeped some, then followed the great hound into the park.

"Something comes," the rat said. Then he too departed, leaving Bridget alone in the sunken room.

Anxiety settled thick around her. Bridget started pacing about, stretching her legs as she worked off her stress. Three times she circled the dugout, taking a nibble of Butch's dog food with each pass. Bridget didn't think much of its taste (the brittle food certainly paled against the things Jessica served that Bridget used to think were so horrible – if only she could chow down on that stuff again!), but this dog food was better than nothing. Bridget wished she hadn't been asleep when this "stumper" had stopped by to refill the hound's bowls. She would have liked to lick his hand.

With each step, though, Bridget found something troubling. She had seen her share of deadwood structures these hairless ones had built, but never one like this – a room where such giants couldn't just walk in and out. But if this dugout was indeed like the other rooms, and she bet it had to be, then somewhere it had to lead to a slope or stairs where giants could come and go without scaling that ledge. That thought cheered her, for if she could find those stairs, she too could get out and be free. But after three circles of her walls, she saw no other passages, which meant the stairs, or whatever, had to be within some neighboring room inside this huge place – and that meant one of these walls must open up, like Jessica's front portal. Bridget just had to find it.

She heard the hawk screech a savage warning. It sounded some ways away. Butch answered from off around the grounds. As twilight settled around them, Edna sprang down to Bridget's side, panting from her hard run. She cheeped, then repeated herself. Bridget shrugged, not knowing what else to do. Frustrated, the squirrel leaped back out, her thick tail flapping in the breeze. She soon returned with a small rat wheezing at her heels.

"She tells me never leave youh," the rat squealed. "She says many cats on the way."

"Many? Does that happen often?"

The squirrel offered rapid chatter. "Only when the humans come," the rat said. "But no humans here, so this is different. And she is concerned; cats always fight. The hawk, he drives away many, but more coming. Too many."

Edna cheeped a lively set of tones. "She says youh should hide. Now."

"Why?" Bridget asked.

Edna scolded them both. "Do not question the elder!" the rat snapped. "Cats fight. Now hide!"

To Bridget's amazement, Edna ran right up the side of the wall to disappear on the roof. But of course, she could do that, the feline reminded herself – she's a squirrel.

"I hide too," the rat said. "Cats hate rats."

Bridget just stood there, looking at him. He stared back. Then they both laughed.

A piercing shriek split the winds. Bridget cringed at the call of Tom'alaxt the hawk. It seemed so close, echoing again and again from around the park.

Butch raced across the tree line, his red coat sparkling, his long fangs aglow in the twilight. He dove into a tall thicket, filling the glade with his terrible barks.

"Crazy, isn't it?"

Bridget trembled at the voice. Scarface!

He sat beside her, the poor rat knocked senseless beneath the warrior's paws.

"I should have known you'd make friends here," he said, batting the little rodent aside.

Bridget watched the body fly and felt like crying. A friend had suffered – because of her.

"How'd you get in here?" she whispered.

"Oh, that was easy. Few things can catch me when I don't want them to. But I must admit, I had some help."

"The other cats...."

"You're smart; I'll give you that. But so am I, squirt. You see, when I realized you'd beguiled Butch and the hawk, well, I knew they'd probably try to stop me. So I had to get them out of the way."

Bridget took a step backward. "Stop you?" she pondered aloud.

"From killing you," Scarface answered, with a tone as friendly as any he'd ever spoken. "It's your fault, really. I did everything I could to just get you out of the way. I didn't want to have to hurt you – by myself, anyway."

"But why? Why do you care – "

"I told you," Scarface snapped, cutting her off. "I was to be Sebastian's successor – not you! I'd waited years for that! And then you just come into my life, a cute little bundle of troublesome joy – just the perfect little kitten. How could I compete with that? I can't, obviously. So I've got to get rid of you."

"But you did!" Bridget cried, backing to the wall.

"Oh, but they know where you are now. They'll be coming for you. So I don't have much time, do I?"

Scarface lunged for her. She dodged to her left, evading him with ease. Still, her legs felt stiff, her chest tight.

Chuckling, he leaped for her again. She feigned left, then went right. But this time Scarface twisted back and dove straight for her head. She ducked. He soared over her, laughing.

Bridget didn't understand him. She'd seen kittens show more finesse!

A bit of acorn shell struck her head. She twisted in anger to view the rooftop when she spied Edna tossing another acorn her way, a whole nut this time. So Bridget tested her legs and jumped atop the bench. Scarface followed, landing with such force that the deadwood construct tumbled beneath them. Rolling away from the wall, the bench landed on its side in the middle of the sunken floor.

When she'd realized what had happened, Bridget could have kissed the little squirrel. Instead, she jumped to a perch on the narrow bench board, and from there she hopped atop the ledge wall with only a tad discomfort.

Darkness settled throughout the woods. The hawk cried high above her, while on the far grass slope Bridget spied a team of rats chasing a cat. The unusual sight

thrilled her.

Something landed hard on her back, pounding her into the earth. Her breath rushed out. Scarface's fangs closed on her spine.

"Sorry, kid," he whispered.

In one quick jerk, Bridget felt Scarface's fearsome weight surge away. Butch was there, growling through a mouth full of calico cat. He shook the feline as he bit down, but Scarface fought back, thrusting his claws into the hound's snout and reaching for his eyes. With a brash sweep of his neck, Butch threw Scarface across the woodlands, then bayed his scariest roar as he charged for the kill. The great warrior cat awaited the onslaught, bolting left at the last moment to leap clear of the dog, and straight for Bridget.

The image horrified her. Butch twisted about as quick as he could in the dead leaves, but Bridget knew Scarface would reach her first. He bore down on her, his eyes burning like torches in the night. Rage consumed him.

Bridget sprinted for the trees, forgetting her wounds and grief. A line of oaks loomed before her. She dove between them and tumbled down the forgotten creek bed. Her back landed in chill water. The sensation sickened her.

Howling in his fury, Scarface tore down the steep slope. Bridget thrashed about in the water, fighting the small current, but even more, she battled her revulsion and deep-set fears of drowning. Her front claws snagged a fallen limb bridging the stream. She latched onto it with her last desperate surge of strength and pulled. It proved enough. With that final effort, she rolled onto the sandy shore.

Scarface towered above her. He bared his fangs – and screamed in terror!

Snapper had found his tail!

Scarface swatted at the turtle's bony head, but Old Snapper just closed his eyes and hung on. Extending his powerful forelegs, the horned turtle started dragging Scarface into the depths.

Before that moment, Bridget had considered the attack cries of hawks and hounds were the worst she'd ever heard. They paled beneath the desperate pleas Scarface made as his tail slid into the stream. Bridget couldn't bear to listen, and yet she knew she couldn't help him, so she crawled away, her pain dwarfed by her shame.

"May God have mercy," she whispered.

A pair of strong hands scooped her from the water's edge. Bridget cried out. It was John! John had come for her! She threw herself at his neck, forgetting all the anguish she'd ever held for the gruff giant. John cuddled her against his shoulder as he stepped with care up the slope, where Jessica waited to surround her beloved cat with tears of joy.

"The Stumper!" cried the rats. "The Stumper!"

Peering between Jessica's arms, Bridget watched Butch go running up to an old hairless giant seated on the severed remains of an oak trunk, its leftover wood cut low to the earth. The great hound rose up, planting a paw on both sides of the aged one's head to lick his face.

"He always does this," the man said, patting the dog's solid chest.

A curious feeling sank into Bridget; she seemed to know that voice, though she

couldn't figure out how or why. Then Jessica nuzzled the cat against her neck, and Bridget forgot all about it.

"Beautiful setter," John said as Butch settled at Jason's feet. "He yours?"

"Him? Oh, no," Jason said. "Golden retriever, actually. He lives here. Kind of an unofficial watchdog. But I tell you, he's the most loving beast you'll ever find. Takes care of all the kids. Every park needs a dog like him." Then he leaned close to John and whispered, "I keep him fed, you know. Every morning – right here, from this stump. Don't tell anyone."

John laughed.

A great splashing echoed from the creek. Bridget cringed.

"Honey," said Jessica, "don't you think we'd better be going home?"

John nodded, but when the old man drew up his cane and staggered down to the water's edge, John followed him. A few moments later they returned, Jason having traded his walking stick for a very wet and timid Scarface.

Bridget recoiled, but then she realized the old warrior had no fight left in him. The soaked feline just clung to the old man's side, not knowing what else to do.

"Poor little thing," Jason said, stroking the shaking cat. "That old snapping turtle almost had him down there."

Jessica stared at Scarface, but said nothing. Her attention and love she saved for Bridget.

"Looks like his tail's broken, and maybe a paw, too," said the old storekeeper. Then he chuckled. "But don't you worry," he told the old cat. "I have a friend who'd just love to see you. Let's go see Pep – shall we? Why not! I'm sure he's expecting me to call right about now, anyway."

Then Jason turned a careful eye to Bridget. "Keep an eye on her a day or two. If she's not eating well, or if her legs stay stiff, you might want to take her down to Dr. Pepper James. Best vet in town. But my guess is you won't need to. I think that dog there cleaned her up pretty good."

Jessica raised Bridget up and kissed her. Bridget nearly swooned from her love.

"Thank you," Jessica whispered.

"Oh, thank you," Jason told her. "You don't know how it makes me feel to see a good animal have a loving home. She's God's gift, you know. You take care of her, and you'll be blessed many times over."

By Kirby Lee Davis

Twenty-four

From that moment on, Bridget was a changed cat.
Oh, she was still cantankerous, feisty, and ever klutzy. She continued to knock off boxes of Bisquick and picture frames, car keys and billfolds. But never again did she lose sight of where her heart lay. She watched over the household for twelve years, helping bring two young girls and a timid little boy into a world of faith, hope, and love. And when, as she breathed her last, she got to see Dr. Jessica Ferguson smile down upon her one last time, full of life and light, with a happy marriage and blossoming family, Bridget knew she had served the Creator well.

Butch spent the rest of his years guarding all who visited the park, wondering all the while what happened to the little warrior who had befriended him. Day by day he watched for her return, but she never did. It saddened him. Then one day the Stumper failed to keep his morning call. In his place came a human that the great retriever somewhat remembered. The soft-spoken man laid a fresh blanket down for Butch in the windmill's storage area and filled his food and water dishes, then stepped over to the stump to feed the squirrels, birds, and others. When Butch rambled to his side, the man tied a shiny gold collar about the dog's neck. As those arms closed around his head, Butch smelled Bridget on the man's coat. With that, the dog was content.

John took the Stumper's place from that day on, and as his kids matured, they joined him. Smelling Bridget on each of these humans, they became Butch's favorites as he fulfilled his time on this earth.

But of all the souls revealed in this book, perhaps Scarface redeemed himself the most. The great cat found his home in the pet shop, clearing out the mice and forging order from the chaos that Jason had always tolerated. Scarface kept the dogs under control, quieted the birds whenever they got restless, and overall maintained his own firm command on everything. Jason soon wondered how he'd ever gotten along without Charles, as he named his beloved cat. Together they finished their years with peace and love, bringing God's joy to everyone they met.

The End

By Kirby Lee Davis

Acknowledgements

First and foremost, I give thanks to my Lord God, from whom all blessings (and story efforts) flow. A deep hug and appreciation go to my loved ones who inspired this project. Special thanks to Katie Keeney, Darla Knight, Nancy Edwards Clay, Pat Stone, Shawna Childers, Robin Stroud, Dana and Lesa Davis, LuAnne Nooe, JoAnne Crown Rogers, Tim Flowers, Kevin Breazile, Matt DeGarcia, Beth Schneider, Jake Dollarhide, and many other friends and family who helped me complete this.

The Tulsa Animal Welfare Shelter deserves a warm note for helping me with several photos. The Tulsa River Parks along the gorgeous Arkansas River provided a wonderful backdrop for many shots. LuAnne and Tim helped stage some desired interior scenes. Matt owns the beautiful dogs pictured in this book. Sasha, the golden retriever, so captured the spirit of Butch that I changed his identity from an Irish settler, my longtime dream pet. Shadow is Matt's oh-so-playful and loving German Shepherd.

My final thanks go to you, the reader! I hope you enjoy this for many years to come. Have a great day!

If you liked this book, check out

godsfurryangels.com!

And look for GFA's companion book, revealing events before, during, and after those told in *God's Furry Angels*!

Add it to your collection!